Julianne's heart started to race with a mix of giddiness and panic. She had just met this guy, and she was already feeling totally swept away. Was she completely crazy? Swimming inside the feeling, Julianne shut her eyes. She felt their bodies move closer to each other, and then his lips touched hers. Julianne felt like she was floating above the beach—watching the moonlight reflecting off the water, the huge expanse of perfectly flat sand, the couple on the ground kissing. It was as if fireworks were exploding everywhere. She felt like the entire beach had been electrified by their kiss.

Books by Hailey Abbott:

FORBIDDEN BOY

✦ ✦ ✦

Hailey
ABBOTT

HARPER TEEN
An Imprint of HarperCollins*Publishers*

HarperTeen is an imprint of HarperCollins Publishers.

Produced by Alloy Entertainment
151 West 26th Street, New York, NY 10001

Library of Congress catalog card number: 2007930290
ISBN 978-0-06-125382-9

Typography by Andrea C. Uva

❖

First Edition

Chapter One

✦

Julianne dragged her feet across the ground, the soles of her worn-in red ballet flats leaving sand trails on the cement behind her. Twenty yards ahead on the beach, Chloe was waiting for her, tapping one platform espadrille impatiently. "Jules, move it or lose it! This party waits for no man!" Julianne squinted to see her sister through the ten o'clock moonlight and shivered as a burst of early-June breeze broke through the warm night and crept up her spine. Around her, the sky was blue-black, and the only things she could make out clearly were the reflection of the water and the shape of the dunes.

Although Chloe's tone was light, Julianne rolled her eyes in her sister's direction and let out an exasperated sigh. She hunched her shoulders, shoved her hands deep into the pockets of her faded Citizens, and grumbled. "It doesn't matter. I'm sure by the time we get there someone will have snatched up the beach rights and we'll have to head back home anyway. I mean, it isn't about who's been here the longest. If some arrogant jerks with buckets of money decide to, oh, I don't know, build a massive addition onto their huge glass house, they can just take over the beach to do that any time they want—right?"

"Oh, Jules . . ." Chloe sighed, lacing her fingers through the belt loops of her denim miniskirt. Julianne noticed that her sister's tangerine manicure matched her braided ribbon belt perfectly. Chloe was obviously trying her best to ignore the recent developments threatening their home. Even though their artist mother had purchased the family's ocean-side property and its cozy 1960s cottage-style house, full of quirky nooks and little balconies nearly thirty years ago, changes in the neighborhood were now threatening to force the family out of their beachside house.

Over the past few years, wealthy families, enchanted by the beauty of the beach, had begun moving into the neighborhood en masse. It seemed that a new mansion was springing up around them practically every month. With each new mansion came a new lawyer knocking on the door trying to cajole, guilt-trip, or bully the family into selling their land so that the new neighbors could build some "really amazing" hot tub, cabana, or heliport on the beach.

"We'll be okay," Chloe continued, turning toward the ocean. "It's been our house for thirty years; no one can take it from us. Mom and Dad had their first date on our beachfront, they got married in the house, we have both lived our entire lives there, and Mom . . . well, you know."

Neither girl wanted to finish Chloe's sentence. Although their mother had been dead for several years, the house was still full of her creativity and warmth.

"I don't know," Julianne protested. "The Moores really mean business. They're way more intense than any of the other families have been." The Moore family had only moved in a few weeks earlier, but they were incredibly vocal about their plans to build a huge addition onto their already massive mansion. "I mean, it's totally insane. They move in, level a whole chunk of the beach, and build this huge glass castle looking out onto the ocean. Okay, whatever, they're not the first. But now they want to build a gigantic addition, too? For what? Servants' quarters? A horse stable? What else could they possibly need?"

"I know. I don't trust them either," Chloe conceded. "But we can't do anything about it tonight, so we might as well enjoy ourselves." They had stopped moving toward the party, and Julianne shivered slightly as a whisper of cool ocean breeze broke through the warmth of the night. Fearing that Jules might turn around and head home, Chloe switched tactics. "Listen, Little Mary Sunshine, we're going to this party and we're going to have a good time—whether you like it or not. It's non-negotiable. So you can enjoy yourself or you can pretend to enjoy yourself, but those are your only options."

"Ooh, don't I get to look behind door number three before I decide?"

"Nope, that's it. You can learn to love it or you can learn to fake it," Chloe chirped, enumerating Julianne's options with her fingers. She looked like a very determined camp counselor trying to wheedle some bratty child into drinking the bug juice. Julianne felt her shoulders relax and couldn't help but let out a short laugh. Laughing felt like gulping huge mouthfuls of air after being underwater for a very long time.

"Okay, then," Julianne conceded. "Sounds like a plan. I can do fun. I love fun. Fun is my middle name."

"Um, Jules?" Chloe swept her hair back off her shoulders and arched one well-maintained eyebrow toward her younger sister. "You don't have a middle name."

Julianne shrugged her shoulders and giggled, noticing Chloe's triumphant expression. "You got me there, Captain Literal. Whose party is this, anyway?"

"Okay. So, do you remember Jess and Molly? From

Kappa Delta?" Chloe had rushed the sorority her first semester at UCLA and already had more friends than Julianne could keep track of. Julianne pursed her lips together, trying to match faces to names. "Anyway," Chloe continued, "it's their old roommate, Kristen. She's great."

"Did she go to high school with you? I don't remember her," Julianne cut in. Chloe always knew everyone, everywhere, and it was generally difficult to keep track of which friends were from which school, job, or club. In the summer in the Pacific Palisades, though, Julianne felt like everyone was friends. Surrounded by sand and sunshine, it was almost impossible not to have fun.

"Nope. I think she went to private school somewhere. I met her during rush. Anyway, she has a bonfire permit, kegs, the whole nine. I'm sure we'll probably know at least half the people there. And . . ." Chloe's voice trailed off as she twisted a strand of coffee-colored hair around her finger.

"And?" Julianne prodded.

Julianne's eyes met Chloe's, both flashing in recognition at the same time. "Oh no," Jules sputtered. "Oh no no no no no."

Chloe shifted her weight and looked at her sister, still twisting her hair. "J, c'mon. You need a distraction from the stress with Dad and the house. You're going to give yourself an ulcer. You're going to give *me* an ulcer."

Julianne threw up her hands in mock indignation, hoping that Chloe would catch the gesture even on the darkened beach. "Me? *I'm* going to give *you* an ulcer?" she mock-whined. "You just took, like, ninety-seven classes; you're working at the children's hospital this summer; you do the expert sudoku for fun; and you just scheduled a bikini wax for Wednesday"—Julianne took an exaggerated breath before finishing her rant—"and *I'm* the thing that's eating away at your stomach lining?"

"Okay, let me rephrase. My ulcer aside, we both know that things have been a little high-intensity on the home front recently." Chloe glanced at her sister for confirmation. "And you know what's a great stress-reliever? Making out."

"So have you already picked someone out to relieve my stress, or do I draw straws when we get there?" Julianne asked grudgingly.

Chloe clapped her hands and reached out to put an arm around her younger sister. "Oh, Jules, he's totally hot. And super smart. You're going to love him."

In the distance, Julianne could hear the thumping bass line of a Common song. She could smell the bonfire smoke and hear the waves chasing the shoreline. Chloe did have a point. Was there anything better than a start-of-summer beach party? She laughed as she let her sister drag her down the beach, over the dunes, and toward the party.

As soon as Chloe and Julianne hit the mass of people weaving around the bonfire, a group of shouting and laughing girls bum-rushed Chloe and pulled her off in pursuit of a keg. Alone in the hive of UCLA Greeks, Santa Monica rugby guys who'd somehow caught a ride over, and assorted skaters, surfers, friends from school, and townies, Julianne felt like she was floating in the middle of a cyclone of activity. She looked out over the firelit field of sun-streaked blond heads and laughed. It was a complete Palisades mélange. To her right, Julianne saw her co-editor of the *Cliffview*–the Palisades High art magazine–snuggled into the lap of the adorable college guy who waited tables over at the Fishtail. On the other side of the bonfire, she could just make out her third-grade science partner (who was now earning a reputation as a pretty decent longboarder). Enthusiastic girls in tiny cutoff sweats and bikini tops were tossing a Frisbee with a group of cute boys in lifeguard sweatshirts, their Billabong surf shorts hanging easily off of their hips. Julianne bopped her head to the beat as the music transitioned into last summer's Rihanna song. Humming "Umbrella, ella . . . ella . . ." to herself, she continued her inaugural party lap.

"Jules!" A chorus of male voices bellowed her name from a distance and, squinting, Julianne could just make out Mitch and Hunter, two of her cross-country teammates, and a few of their friends, up ahead.

"Hey there!" She sidled up to her teammates, arms thrown wide open to receive their bear hugs. "How's summer treating you so far?"

The guys shrugged their muscular shoulders before answering. "Oh, you know. Some surfing, some running, just trying to chill a little before work starts," Mitch replied in his laid-back surfer drawl.

Hunter nodded in agreement, his sandy curls bobbing. "And you, J-money? Big summer plans? Are you still working with Bill?"

Julianne nodded. "Yes, indeedy."

"Rock on. Me too." Mitch smiled, his huge dimples on display. "And Hunt might be popping by for a few jobs. The pay is sweet."

Julianne grinned, delighted that she'd be spending a summer in the sun with some of her favorite boys. "Awesome. It's a cool project, too. I think we're going to have a blast. In, you know, that manual-labor type of way."

"Works for me!" the guys chimed at the same time.

"Hey," Hunter started hopefully. "Jules, have you heard from Kat lately?"

Kat Tse, Julianne's best friend, had briefly dated Hunter over the spring and they were still friends. "Nope, not in a few days," Julianne replied, shaking her head. "I think she's still settling into her dorm in Madrid. Her Spanish classes don't start until next week."

"Cool. When you talk to her, tell her I said hey," Hunter said easily. Julianne admired his comfort level with Kat. Although she was still friendly with most of her exes, she definitely didn't count them among her nearest and dearest.

"Will do." Julianne grinned and nodded.

"We should head out," Mitch said. "I've got to be up early tomorrow. Fishing with my dad. And these losers"—he gestured to the other guys—"all need rides home."

"Have a good night," Julianne said, doling out a parting round of hugs. "See you at work."

"Totally." Hunter grinned. As the guys headed away down the beach, he turned around and called over his shoulder, "Oh, Jules, Lucy is looking for you. She has your negatives or something. You left them at the Mean Bean."

"Awesome. Thanks. Later, guys." Julianne waved at her friends, filled her lungs with delicious salty air, and headed off in search of her favorite self-proclaimed "coffee-shop wench."

After fifteen minutes of searching for Lucy and the envelope of negatives she'd left at the Mean Bean the day before, Julianne was still empty-handed. She had, however, taken a few mini-breaks to admire the surfers peeling off their T-shirts to go night-swimming, and to say hello to a few more friends from school. She was having a fabulous time, but she was just plain thirsty.

"'Scuse me." Julianne edged past a blond couple dancing so close they could have been sharing a kidney, en route to the first cooler she could find. Scooting past hordes of tanned bodies bumping up against each other, she unconsciously tugged down the hem of her soft gray T-shirt. Julianne smiled, looking down at the fabric. She had forgotten how smeared and spotted with black ink it was. All of the stains were like birthmarks, giving the shirt uniqueness and character. She loved this shirt, even though Chloe rolled her eyes and pouted whenever she came down the stairs wearing it. It was Julianne's shirt for getting things done, for creating new things, for making life happen. And, as worn as it was, it was still her favorite party shirt. She scooped her long dark curls off of her neck and into a messy bun atop her head in preparation for a dive toward the cooler. Moments later, she was walking away with a can of PBR—the official beer of the perpetually broke and self-consciously hip—in her hand, and a trail of cooler water down the front of her favorite shirt. She was congratulating herself on a job well done when she felt a hand on her shoulder. Julianne wheeled around.

"Thank God—I thought I'd completely lost you." Chloe's face was flushed from the bonfire, her green hoodie unzipped to reveal a dusty pink tank top trimmed with funky antique lace. "Are you having fun yet?"

"Totally," Julianne conceded.

"Fantastic!" Chloe bubbled, linking her arm through Jules's and pulling her along. "It's about to get even better." Chloe swept Julianne through the crowd, back past the bonfire, in between two lines of coolers, and around what appeared to be two dueling sororities engaged in a full-on dance war, before stopping at the kegs.

Julianne motioned to her nearly full can of PBR. "I'm all set." Chloe nudged her and tilted her head toward a keg about fifteen feet away. A guy, probably Chloe's age, was dangling above it, upside down, supported by his friends.

"That's Michael," Chloe announced, like she was showing off a prize pig at a state fair. Julianne followed Chloe's meaningful stare in the direction of the airborne hottie without making any sort of connection.

"Who's Michael?" Chloe widened her eyes and arched her eyebrows as though Julianne had just asked her where babies came from. "Oh, right." The pieces snapped together in Julianne's mind. "The stress-reliever. Gotcha."

Michael flipped down off the keg and charged toward Chloe and Julianne, one arm outstretched, calling out, "Chloe! My favorite lab partner!" as he approached. Michael was tall and tan. His chest muscles were clearly outlined under the two coordinating J.Crew polo shirts he had layered one atop the other—both collars standing pertly at attention. His blond hair was messy, sticking up in post-keg-stand chaos, and his brown eyes were like dishes of melting chocolate. Well-worn khaki cargo pants hung off of his massive quadriceps. He looked just like all the rest of Chloe's frat friends—definitely hot, but a little too aware of his hotness to be Julianne's type.

"Michael, this is my sister, Julianne." Chloe beamed once he was standing at her side. "Jules, this is Michael. He was in my physics section last semester. I never would have made it through without him."

Michael grinned and rolled his eyes. "Your sister is full of it. She practically wrote the textbook. She put the rest of us premed dorks to shame." Chloe flipped her hand at him dismissively. Julianne knew that Chloe could run circles around anyone in a math or science class. Or graph circles around them. Whatever it was that physicists actually did.

"Her modesty is only part of her charm." Julianne laughed, teasing her sister. "Nice to meet you." She extended her hand toward Michael for a handshake and was surprised when he pulled her into a hug. "Chloe's told me a lot about that class," Jules said, recovering her composure.

"Really?" Michael asked incredulously.

"Nope. Actually, not at all. Unless—wait . . . did the TA have a faux-hawk and a fantastic butt?"

"I'm more of a bowl-cut guy myself, so I didn't really notice. Sorry 'bout that." He chuckled at his own joke.

While he spoke, Julianne glanced behind him. A pack of identical frat boys, all clad in the same polo shirts, khaki pants, and rumpled hairstyles as Michael, were approaching quickly from the bonfire.

"Dude, where'd you go?" One of the guys clapped a beefy hand onto Michael's back.

"Yeah, dude, you disappeared," another one echoed, punching him in the shoulder. Julianne caught Chloe's eye, and the sisters stifled a giggle.

Michael gestured toward Julianne and Chloe. "Guys, this is Chloe, my lab partner from last semester, and this is her sister, Julianne."

Julianne said hello and smiled, but walked away as quickly as her round-toed slip-ons would allow in the sand.

"What's wrong?" Chloe asked, following her. "Didn't you like Michael? He's such a sweet guy. And check out his arms."

"No, he was fine," Julianne answered, taking a lap around the kegs. "He was cute—just like every single guy you know is cute—but he wasn't really my type. Besides, I want to try to catch up with some more people from school before they start leaving. You know, try to make plans before we all start working. But he *was* really cute. And I think he may have been interested in talking about more than lab with you."

Chloe's eyes sparkled. "Really? You think? But I was

really hoping that you guys might, you know, hit it off tonight."

Julianne, detecting the sparkle of interest in Chloe's voice, grinned at her sister. "Go for it. You should definitely go for it," she encouraged. "Besides, you always tell me that you have excellent taste . . ."

Chloe giggled but didn't have a chance to answer. As she opened her mouth to speak, a skinny brown-haired guy came hurtling across the beach—propelled by the force of someone's sloppy keg-stand dismount—and tumbled directly into her, knocking her down with him.

The brown-haired guy panted, "Good to know that gravity's still working." He turned to Chloe. "Are you okay?" Chloe nodded, clearly a little dazed, and dusted the sand off of her denim skirt. He shifted his gaze to Julianne and smiled. "How about you? I didn't take you out, too, did I?"

"Nope. Still standing. Are *you* okay?" She smiled at him, pulled her hair out of its bun, and let the curls spill down her back.

The reflection from the bonfire lit his face and his dark eyes shimmered. Julianne felt a flash of jealousy. There was a part of her that really wished that this skinny, possibly-concussed stranger had managed to land right smack on top of *her* instead of her sister.

The brown-haired guy's mouth was pasted into a perfect half smile. She felt like she was in the middle of every single musical where the dancing stops and the star is suddenly backlit by one huge glowing spotlight.

"Yeah, fine. Who knows? Maybe this is the start of a promising career in roller derby?" He had one of those wry, almost winking, smiles. He was tall, skinny without being gawky, but definitely a little bit awkward in a really endearing way. Julianne wanted to tousle his hair or make sure he drank enough milk. His eyes were huge—dark and fluid.

"Hey, Crash," she joked. "Do you have a name?"

He blushed. "Oh, God. I'm sorry. First I plow over your friend, then I'm flat-out rude. I'm Remi."

"Remi, huh? Cool name." Julianne held her hand out to him. "Julianne. And you just met my sister, Chloe. She looks different upright, though." She gestured to Chloe, who was fixing her hair and talking to unfortunate-keg-stand guy and Michael, who had rushed over to make sure she was okay. Remi saluted in Chloe's direction.

"Way to make an entrance!" Chloe called back in their direction.

Remi looked sheepishly at Julianne and smiled. She felt time start slipping into cinematic slow motion again and grasped for some sort of normal human social question to ask next. "Do you, um, live around here?" she stammered.

"Seattle, actually." Over his shoulder, the waves were crashing against the beach.

"Oh." Julianne felt her throat closing. She'd known this guy for maybe thirty seconds, but the thought of him not being in LA this summer made her queasy.

"Yeah, I'm in school up there. But I'm around for the summer. My parents just moved here." Julianne felt herself relax instantly. "Are you from the area?" he asked. Julianne thought she detected hopefulness in his voice.

"Unfortunately." Julianne laughed and rolled her eyes in the direction of a group of girls, each doing a variation on the same Malibu Barbie impression, struggling to form a human pyramid a few feet away. "No, actually I love it here. Just don't judge all of us by the Pussycat Dolls over there."

"Maybe you could show me around sometime? Save me the effort of having to get to know the place better all by myself before I get the wrong idea?" Remi paused. "I mean, if you don't have too much going on this summer."

"Sure. I can do the tour with my eyes closed. No human pyramid, though." They laughed, and Julianne felt her entire body filling with warmth. She knew she was beaming like an idiot. At least she wasn't the only one. She'd never felt this comfortable talking to someone before, and yet so awkward at the same time. Somehow, talking to Remi was like breathing. She wasn't sure she would know how to stop. She was pretty sure that she didn't want to. Remi and Julianne made eye contact again, grinning at each other like fools. Faces illuminated by the moonlight and the distant bonfire, they stared at each other until it felt like time had completely stopped.

Suddenly, Julianne felt a hand on her back and whipped around. "Sorry to break up the party," Chloe said, rubbing her temples, "but I have a headache and need to go home. Jules, can you drive?"

"Oh God, was it—" Remi started, but Chloe cut him off.

"No worries," she assured him. "I've taken worse falls than that. Besides, Michael's buying me dinner tomorrow to make up for it. These frat guys have loyalty down to a science, huh?" Chloe grinned. "Anyway, it was good running into you. Get it? Running into you? Oh God, I actually said that out loud. I need to go home." Chloe started off down the beach toward the car.

"Okay, well, see you around." Julianne looked down at the ground. She could barely breathe.

"Okay. Well, I guess I'll see you." Remi's voice was barely audible, his shoulders sloping downward.

Jules felt like her heart was being ripped out of her chest, but she tossed her shoulders back, laced her fingers through her belt loops, and straightened her back as she started to walk away. Fifty yards down the beach she heard Remi's voice.

"Hey, Julianne!" Remi was suddenly right beside her

again, breathing heavily after his sprint. "You forgot this." He tucked a scrap of paper into her hand. "My phone number." Not smooth—definitely not smooth—but very cute. "You know, in case your sister needs it for health insurance or whatever. And so you can give me that tour. It's hard work getting jaded on your own, you know." He grinned.

"Definitely." She smiled back. "I wouldn't want to leave you hanging."

Remi's face softened as he stared right into Julianne's eyes. She felt like he could actually see inside her head—that somehow, effortlessly, they already understood each other. Softly, he put his hand on the side of her face and Julianne felt like the spot was on fire. Her heart started to race with a mix of giddiness and panic. She had just met this guy, and she was already feeling totally swept away. Was she completely crazy? Swimming inside the feeling, Julianne shut her eyes. She felt their bodies move closer to each other, and then his lips touched hers. Julianne felt like she was floating above the beach—watching the moonlight reflecting off the water, the huge expanse of perfectly flat sand, the couple on the ground kissing. It was as if fireworks were exploding everywhere. She felt like the entire beach had been electrified by their kiss.

"I'm sorry—I'm really, really sorry," Julianne murmured, breaking out of Remi's arms. "I have to go. I don't know where Chloe went, and I don't know if she's okay. I need to find her." Julianne's throat was dry. It was like the very worst part of every fairy tale. Suddenly she was Cinderella at midnight. "I'll call you, I promise." She flashed the scrap of paper with a triumphant smile before taking off down the beach in search of her sister.

Julianne drifted toward the small parking lot where they'd left the car a few hours earlier, calling Chloe's name over and over. She couldn't stop thinking about the kiss. It had just felt so *meant to be* somehow. A guy she had never seen before had literally fallen right into her lap—okay, well, her sister's lap, but close enough—at the start of the summer, on the beach she loved.

And he wasn't just any guy. Julianne couldn't put her finger on it, but there was something special about Remi. As she scanned the tiny parking lot, she made a mental note to give Chloe some "I told you so" points for dragging her out to this party.

Out of the corner of her eye, Julianne saw Chloe sitting on the ground, leaning against the bumper of their car, her head resting next to a faded "Imagine Whirled Peas" bumper sticker that their dad had stuck on. Julianne crept over and put her hand on Chloe's shoulder. "Chloe," she said softly, kneeling next to her sister. "Sorry I disappeared, I was just . . . saying goodbye to someone. C'mon, let's go."

Chloe opened her eyes, and turned to face Julianne.

"Not so fast, Missy. You were so *not* just giving out casual goodbyes. Look at you—you're glowing! I can even see it in the dark with major head trauma! Tell me everything."

Julianne smiled. She couldn't stop beaming. "I think this will tell you everything you need to know," she intoned dramatically as she dug her hand into her right pocket to show Remi's phone number to Chloe. But all she felt was the fabric. She could have sworn it was in there. She reached into her left pocket and came up empty-handed again. Horrified, she thought back to saying goodbye to Remi. Suddenly, she realized that she'd never put the paper in her pocket. She had been holding it when she dashed off. Now, clearly, she wasn't clutching the little scrap of paper anymore. She must have dropped it on the beach. Julianne felt her heart drop to the sand as she helped Chloe into the passenger seat of the Toyota hybrid they were sharing this summer. She thought she was going to be sick.

How could she be so upset—she'd just met the guy— at a beach party of all places. Maybe she'd been taken in by the bonfire, the PBR, and the view from the beach.

But even as she tried to rationalize, Julianne knew there was more to it. She knew that if she didn't find some way to see Remi again, she would be losing out on something really wonderful.

"I wouldn't worry too much, Jules," Chloe murmured sleepily. "If he's your Prince Charming, he'll find his way back. He has to, actually. I think it's in the job description." But Julianne barely heard her.

The sisters drove home in silence. Chloe napped with her head pressed against the cool car window. And Julianne tried to fight back her growing disappointment. She had just met an amazing guy who she would probably never see again.

This did not bode well for her summer.

Chapter Two

✦

Julianne felt the sun streaming in her bedroom window and rolled over, burying her head in a smooshy pillow. She had been having such completely blissful, vivid dreams that she didn't want to nudge herself back into reality, no matter how glorious the California morning was. She glanced at her alarm clock—it was almost noon. She'd meant to be up at 9:30, but she just hadn't been able to tear herself out of dream world. She rolled over again, pressing her face directly into the folds of her pillow and breathing in the last lingering remnants of the lavender linen spray that Chloe always spritzed around on laundry days. The new Regina Spektor album was drifting out of her stereo alarm clock, and Julianne allowed herself to drift along with the dreamy melodies until she fully gave into consciousness. With one last sleepy sigh, she pushed herself upright and swung her legs off the side of the bed. Julianne stood up and stretched, raising her hands over her head and arching her back, trying to shake the sleep from her joints. Remi had been in every single one of her dreams, and each had been sweeter and more romantic than the last. Julianne wrapped her arms around herself, as though her cozy room somehow had a chill without Remi in it. She walked over to her closet and pulled a shrunken UCLA hoodie over her head. Shaking out the curls that caught in the hood, Julianne crossed the room again, sat down at her desk, and glanced at her perpetually-on MacBook. Quickly, she dashed off a MySpace message to Kat in Spain.

> K—
> *Met a guy! Ridiculously hot, seriously funny. This is a biggie, I can just tell. Keep your fingers crossed for me! Waves have been amazing all week—wish you were here. Send pictures from Madrid as soon as you have 'em. Oh, and Hunter says hey . . .*
> *xoxo*
> —J

Julianne got up from her desk and pushed the gauzy curtains back from the bay window door that led out to her balcony. She slipped on her flip-flops, unlocked the door, and padded outside. Before her eyes even adjusted to the light, Jules felt the sun beating down on her, making her sweatshirt unnecessary, and heard the lapping of the waves up against the shoreline. She walked over to the railing and leaned against it, watching the waves swell and crash. She allowed herself to drift into a few more moments of morning reverie before looking down onto the beach, which was practically glowing in the late-morning sunshine. Specks of shells caught the light and reflected like tiny prisms, casting even more light across the sand. A few sunbathers dotted the thin strip of sand directly in front of the water. People were scattered in beach chairs and on blankets, thumbing through newspapers or glossy paperback novels under the shade of palm trees.

Jules stared out across the beach and wondered if Remi was sitting on the beach somewhere. She wondered what sort of books he read, what he did for fun, where he hung out. She imagined sitting next to Remi on a towel, him glancing over her shoulder as she sketched fellow beachgoers. Just imagining the closeness made Julianne blush—and she hadn't even gotten around to picturing him in his bathing suit yet!

Three distant but sharp beeps snapped her out of her daydream and she looked up, annoyed. Three hundred yards away she could see a yellow bulldozer moving around at the Moores' place. Did these people have to ruin everything? Julianne shook her head and turned her attention back to the ocean, allowing herself to be soothed by the light sparkling off the waves. Then her father's voice drifted up from the deck below, so she headed back inside to get ready for her day.

After a quick change, Julianne was sitting with her father and Chloe downstairs. "Excuse me, miss. Can I get a refill?" Dad pushed his empty lemonade glass across the glass patio table toward his daughters.

Julianne rolled her eyes in mock exasperation. "First you want sunblock, then you want the umbrella down." She pointed to the oversize blue-and-yellow umbrella jutting out of the middle of the table like a Technicolor palm tree. "And now you want refills? I bet you're not even going to tip. . . ."

Refilling her father's glass from a huge, blown-glass pitcher, she turned her eyes back to the beach in front of her. It was a perfect early-summer afternoon—hot without being humid, the sun the color of butter.

"I've got a tip for you—don't quit your day job." Edward Kahn chuckled softly to himself, pulling Jules's attention back. "You have many talents, Julianna Banana, but waitressing isn't one of them."

Chloe reached across Julianne, grabbing a piece of corn on the cob. "Good thing you decided not to fill out that singing-waitress application at Nifty Fifties then, huh?" she teased.

Julianne practically wrapped herself around the umbrella post in pursuit of the potato salad and sloppily scooped a helping onto her neon plastic plate. "Alas, no roller skates and poodle skirts for me this summer. Just fresh air and building things."

Chloe sat up straight in her chair and squinted through her giant gold-rimmed sunglasses. "Speaking of building things, what's going on over there?" She jerked her thumb toward the construction equipment gathered around the new neighbors' property. All sorts of destructive-looking vehicles were lined up around the house.

Julianne followed her sister's gaze with one eye while monitoring her dad's face with the other. "Beats me. I heard some construction noise when I was out on the balcony before, but that's it. Dad?"

"Nuuhmuh." Dad shrugged between mouthfuls of fruit salad.

"Come again?" Chloe asked.

"I said, 'Nothing much,'" their father repeated. "It's the same thing that always happens. People move here for a summer kingdom and start building their castle. They'll get bored and go back home soon enough." He leaned over the side of his chair to pick up a grape that had escaped his grasp and wedged itself between the wood slats of the deck.

"The bulldozers don't strike me as a sign of boredom," Chloe started, shaking her head.

"They showed up last month, immediately dug a foundation, and erected this crazy greenhouse-looking thing. It looks like they're trying to expand down toward the beach now." Julianne glanced over at the mess of Tonka trucks come alive. From a few hundred yards away they almost looked like a bunch of mechanical bees swarming around a big glass hive.

"Can they do that? Just keep going and going like that?" Julianne wondered out loud.

"Yeah," Chloe added incredulously. "If they keep moving at this rate, they're going to plow that whole stretch of beach right under."

"In a few weeks, they'll decide it's all more trouble than it's worth and sell the property for twice what they paid for it. Just wait. Don't lose any sleep over it, girls. It'll be fine," their father assured them. "But, speaking of sleep, it was nice of you to wake up and join us for lunch, Julianne . . ." he continued slyly.

In the distance, Julianne could hear kids laughing as they rushed up to the water's edge and dashed away, squealing, as soon as the tide approached. *Wow, I can't believe he noticed . . .* she thought.

Chloe said as much out loud. "Gosh, Jules, you must have been out cold to make *Dad* notice you snoozing the morning away. He's been in his studio all day. Way to make your absence known. Hmm . . . I *wonder* what you possibly could have been dreaming about until almost noon . . ." Julianne could hear the slightest shade of glee coloring her sister's voice. She was right, though. Their father, a children's book author, was pretty single-minded writing. Mom had always joked that if she hadn't illustrated his books, her husband would have forgotten who she was entirely while he was writing.

Abruptly changing the subject, Chloe burst out with, "Hey, didn't the Moores come over with their surveyor practically first thing when they moved in?"

"Chloe, don't get all worked up over nothing," Dad said. "Both of you girls worry too much. The neighborhood might be changing, but it doesn't mean much for us. Well, except for longer, meaner lines in the supermarket," he added, winking. "The Moores aren't going to win any conservation awards for building up all that ground, but their crazy glass mansion won't really affect us."

Well, if Dad isn't worried, I won't worry, Julianne thought to herself. She glanced over at Chloe and saw her sister's shoulders starting to ease their way down toward their typical relaxed height. "Nothing to worry about," Julianne said softly, right as something went whizzing through her sight line, smacking Chloe directly on the forehead. Julianne and Chloe whipped their heads toward the opposite side of the table, where their father was chuckling quietly, fingers still poised from flicking a particularly round grape at Chloe's head.

"Now *there's* something to worry about," he declared before the table broke out into an all-out grape-shooting gallery.

Julianne shook her head, grinning, and reached for her camera just in time to catch a few great shots of her crazy family in action.

"No, here's something to worry about—the invasion of the hot summer guys! It looks like our Jules is already halfway to being beamed up." Chloe giggled.

"Not even a little," Julianne fibbed gamely. "It's only June. A girl needs to keep her summer options open until the Fourth of July, at least." She enjoyed keeping the excitement of a new romance quiet for a little while—it made it even more special.

"I like that rule." Chloe nodded thoughtfully. "Saving your fireworks until after the fireworks. Very classy. Besides, you're going to be working at cute-guy headquarters this summer. And you're going to be the only girl there. We'll need some sort of complex rating system to sort through all your options."

"My little girls are growing up. I don't think I like this," Dad muttered pitifully. "One day it's tea parties and art classes, the next it's boys, boys, and more boys."

"Oh, *Daaad*!" Julianne and Chloe groaned in unison, rolling their eyes.

"Jules, sweetie, I don't know how you're going to hold down a job if you're in the habit of sleeping until noon," Dad teased.

"I wouldn't say that sleeping in once constitutes a habit," Julianne protested.

"Not a habit, per se." Chloe smirked. "At least not yet. Wait until you run into that guy again; then we can start predicting recurrences."

"Thank you, Captain Statistical Analysis," Julianne shot back. "After that, maybe you can set up a formal experiment. I can be your very own live-in lab rat. Anyway, I'm going to be spending the entire summer number one, painting, and number two, surrounded by the aforementioned hot guys. I think I'll find it in my heart to pull myself out of bed and get to work somehow." Julianne pulled her oversize sunglasses down her nose and cast a dramatic look at her older sister.

"Point taken," Chloe admitted, laughing. "Honestly, Jules, I can't think of anyone else who could make working on a construction site sound so . . . appealing."

"Are you kidding me? It's going to be fantastic! Sunshine, boys, making things and then painting them? I can't wait to start!" Jules gushed.

"And I," Chloe cut in, not-so-subtly redirecting the conversation, "can't wait to hear more about this guy you met last night. Tell me everything already!"

Julianne felt her cheeks turning red, in a physical

flashback to the night before.

"Chloe, stop picking on your sister," Dad interceded halfheartedly.

"Daaaaa-aad!" Chloe practically squealed. "Don't even! You know you want to know almost as much as I do!"

Chuckling, their father admitted, "You know, I'm not sure that's true. It's just that I'll lose my parenting license if I don't tell you to cut it out at least twice a day. Carry on, then." He smiled, picked up his plate, and headed back into the house.

Chloe lazily swatted at a seagull that was flying perilously close to her plate. His bird buddies squawked overhead, egging him on to fight. Glad of the distraction, Julianne reached under her seat and came back up with her camera—a huge old Nikon SLR. She loved adjusting the lenses and checking the light meter. She snapped away as Chloe took off a flip-flop and threatened to bat at the renegade bird, muttering, "Rats with wings. They're just big rats with wings."

As the seagulls scattered, Chloe turned her attention back to the still-blushing Julianne. "Are you going to spill or not?"

"I don't have any idea what you're talking about," Julianne replied tartly, putting her camera down and lobbing a look of wide-eyed innocence at her sister.

"Oh my God. You're totally gone for this guy!" Chloe was now in full squealing mode. "Jules has a boyfriend! Jules has a boyfriend!"

"Um, excuse me?" Jules interjected. "Which one of us has the hot dinner date with her hot lab partner tonight? Boyfriend, *what*?"

"Seriously, though, Jules. Things looked pretty intense last night. I haven't seen you click with a guy like that in . . . well . . . *ever*," Chloe prompted, her voice more serious.

Julianne smiled to herself, remembering the electrified kiss on the beach, and gave up being vague. "I know. It's true. Talking to him just seemed so natural, Chloe. Like everything fit."

"He *was* pretty cute." Chloe nodded, popping another grape into her mouth.

"And not just that," Julianne continued, her pace quickening. "He was completely hilarious and nice and smart. He was just . . ." Her voice trailed off as she searched for the words. "He was perfect."

Chloe slid her sunglasses off of her face and smiled, her eyes twinkling as she lifted her lemonade glass in a toast. "Well, then, here's to a perfect summer."

"Here, here!" Julianne chimed in.

Chapter Three

✦

Julianne felt like she was being baked alive. The three o'clock sun was beating down, and she could feel it sizzling behind her dark curls. Even with her hair back in a messy bun, tied away from her face with a bandana, she could feel the heat sinking into her skull. She fanned herself with her hand and waited for a burst of cool breeze to come up off the ocean. Two feet away, her black Reef flip-flops lay messily where she had kicked them off, and she sank her toes farther into the sand. She had been out on the beach painting for the last hour, and still had a couple hours to go. Her mother had come out to the beach every day in the summers from two to five—at least until she got too sick to leave the house—to catch the sun on its way back down from the middle of the sky. Hannah Kahn had always said that her greatest pleasure as an artist was to catch the sun on its descent toward the horizon. The shadows were better. There was more depth, more variation. She never wore sunglasses when she painted, because she wanted to see the light in as pure a way as possible. Despite their many similarities, today Jules was definitely not *feeling* her mom's artistic process. It was a gorgeous day, and all she could think about was getting in the water.

Usually, making art chilled Julianne out, but today she was surprisingly distracted. The anniversary of her mother's death was coming up, and Julianne really wanted to have this painting finished by the time it rolled around. It was a challenge for her to paint in her mother's lush, representational style, though. Julianne's work was generally more abstract. She usually loved working in mixed media, but she felt compelled to do this painting her mom's way—to experience the way her mom ticked as an artist. Trying to channel her mom's method was a huge struggle for her, but Julianne desperately wanted to make this painting work.

Today, however, as sweat beaded across her forehead and Lily Allen's voice bounced out of her iPod, Jules felt like she was fighting a losing battle. She just couldn't focus. Her mind kept floating across the beach. When the breeze came up off the water, she was in heaven. She stuck the end of her paintbrush in her messy bun for safekeeping and walked around the canvas, first clockwise, then counterclockwise. She picked up her easel and shuffled a few feet to the left, then to the right again. Julianne wiped her paint-covered hands on the front of her Bermuda shorts and sighed. It felt so much more natural to just take a photo—everything was captured instantly, beautifully, looking exactly like what it was, only better. The water looked perfectly crisp and inviting, and the surfer guys dotting the waves didn't look half bad either. Julianne quickly pulled off her shorts and tank top, revealing her new green Betsey Johnson bikini. She tossed her clothes and bandana on top of her Reefs, set her paintbrush down on her easel, and ran for the water.

The second Jules's toes hit the salt water, she felt her good mood come rushing back to her. She walked in up to her waist, then ducked down, letting the waves rush up to her shoulders, cooling her down instantly. She swam out a few feet and bobbed around, surveying the scene. Some guys from town were tossing a football by the edge of the water, trying not to take out the occasional low-flying seagull. On either side of her, surfers were flexing their strong arms and pushing up onto their boards before gracefully gliding to shore. Mixed in with the boys, Julianne was happy to see some girls representing out on the waves. *Maybe this will be the summer I step up my own surf skills*, Julianne thought. Chloe had always been more the swimmer and surfer in the family, while Julianne spent most of her time on the beach running or sketching. She was a strong enough swimmer and, more often than not, she was able to push up, stay up, and ride in on her board. But Jules knew she'd never really spent the time it takes to get really good at surfing. Kat, who was an amazing surfer, always said it was a shame Julianne didn't spend more time on her board; she swore the cutest guys were always surfers. The group laughing and shouting to Jules's left served as proof. If she could up her skills by the time Kat returned from Madrid, her best friend would be so impressed. Julianne made a mental note to add some surfing time to her summer to-do list.

Beyond the cluster of hot surfers, Julianne noticed a red ponytail whipping behind a girl on a longboard. Jules only knew one person in the Palisades with that fiery hair. *"Lucy!"* She called out to her friend, but the crashing of a wave swallowed her voice. Julianne's mind flashed back to her search for Lucy and her lost negatives at the party the other night. As much as she'd been hoping to find her friend, Julianne didn't regret what she'd done instead one bit. *I wonder if Remi surfs,* she thought dreamily.

Julianne laughed at herself, dunking her head underwater. Why couldn't she stop thinking about Remi? He had been in her head constantly since he'd hurtled into Chloe at high speed. Jules had never felt something click like that so instantly. And the way he'd looked at her right before she ran off . . . Her stomach twisted into a million pretzels just thinking about it. He had looked at her the way she looked through her camera at a perfect shot—transfixed, amazed, like he could suddenly see everything clearly. Talking to Remi was the most fun she'd had in months—and she liked to think that she had a pretty awesome time, generally speaking. Their banter had been so breezy and electric. And now all she wanted was to pick up where they'd left off.

Well, Julianne figured, *no point in trying to avoid reality.* She shook her head to herself. Although the realization made her vaguely sick, she couldn't deny that seeing Remi might have been a one-time deal. Refusing to sulk on such a beautiful day, she paddled back into the crowd of laughing surfers and swimmers, feeling the sun warming her back through the water. Her muscles already loose from her swim, Jules stretched her arms as far as they could go, reaching out for the perfect slicing stroke and shooting through the water. About twenty yards out, she stopped swimming and bobbed up in the cool surf, waiting for the swell of waves behind her. Since she didn't have a surfboard with her, she figured she would just ride waves toward the shore for a while, then ask to borrow someone's board once she got the hang of it. As she heard the familiar roll of an approaching wave, Julianne began stroking forward, gaining speed as the wave did. The growing wall of water caught up to her back and pushed her toward the beach. As the white bubbles of the breaking wave crashed over and around her, Julianne shot back up into the sunshine, exhilarated. Grinning, she swam out into the deeper water to wait for another run.

Bobbing under the water from time to time as she swam out, Julianne was so immersed in the adrenaline rush that she barely felt her body collide with the board of another surfer waiting for a wave.

"Oops. Sorry about that, I'm a newbie," Julianne apologized, laughing at her awkward collision and wiping water out of her eyes as she looked up. When she saw the face of the board's owner, her jaw dropped.

"Oh my God!" It couldn't be. It was just too surreal. She'd met this guy for five perfect minutes at a party, and now he was popping up again the next day? These things only happened to Cinderella.

Remi's eyes were the size of silver dollars and his eyebrows were knitted together in confusion. He was wearing board shorts, and his hair was still damp from his last dunk. He sat astride his surfboard with his bare calves dangling into the water, and his fingers absentmindedly drumming on the board's surface. Jules realized with a shock of adrenaline that he'd been in the pack of surfers she'd been admiring earlier. He kept opening his mouth mechanically but no sounds came out.

"Um. Wow. Um. Just . . . um . . . wow. What are you doing here?" Julianne stammered.

Remi opened and closed his mouth a few more times. He looked like a goldfish reaching for his fishy-flakes. A particularly hot goldfish.

"Are you okay? Are you lost? Are you suffering from sunstroke?" she went on, half-laughing, and fully hoping that she wasn't hallucinating from the sun herself.

"I'm, uh, fine. Totally fine. Just . . . surprised." Remi recovered quickly, running his fingers through his dark hair. Even squinting into the sun, his eyes were huge and liquid.

"Yeah, me too. If I remember correctly, you don't usually make your big entrances upright." Jules laughed, trying to play it cool even though her heart and her stomach were tumbling over each other and leapfrogging up into her throat.

Remi blushed, which of course made Julianne blush. He looked slightly off his game—antsy and utterly unaccustomed to the sun after a long, gray, Seattle spring. Even in the bone-melting heat, Julianne felt a chill run up her spine.

"Were you . . . ?" Remi's voice trailed off, but Julianne followed his eyes toward the shore and knew what he was asking.

"Yeah, actually. Do you . . . ?" She laughed and tipped her head back toward the beach.

"Sure." Remi beamed, sliding off his board and back into the cool water.

As they swam toward the sand, Julianne was delighted that talking to Remi still came just as easily as it had at the Malibu party.

"The waves were awesome today," Remi noted happily.

"They've been beautiful so far this summer," Jules agreed. "It's a good sign."

"Is there some sort of Palisades folklore about what you can learn from a summer of good waves? Some sort of Southern Californian old wives tale?" Remi teased.

"Oh, yeah, definitely." Julianne played along. "See how the waves are more rounded today?" Remi stopped paddling and looked to either side of him before nodding. "That means there's only a fifty percent chance of a shark attack," Julianne intoned dramatically before making a sudden grab for his arm. Startled, Remi let out a yelp. "Gotcha!" Julianne winked.

Remi laughed and splashed Julianne with an armful of water. "You learn something new every day around here." He winked back before hefting himself onto his board and beginning to paddle. "Race you to shore!"

As Julianne and Remi walked out of the ocean and onto the beach, seawater trailing from their hair down their backs, Julianne pointed out some of the Palisades beach highlights. "Over there is where the Labor Day carnival used to be held every summer." She pointed to a pier about a hundred yards down the beach. "Now it's held on the boardwalk by the Fishtail. Have you been to the Fishtail yet?" Remi shook his head. "Oh, you definitely have to check it out. Everyone hangs out there in the summer. They have awesome live music. Let me know if you want to check out a show or something," she finished shyly, casting her eyes toward the sand under her feet. "Oh! And over there . . ." Julianne started the tour back up again, her enthusiasm for the beach and for her town overwhelming any awkwardness. She pointed up the beach toward a cliff, under which a bunch of younger kids were playing Ultimate Frisbee. "When we were in elementary school, we would have our 'girls-only club' meetings in the rocks under those cliffs. The 'boys-only club' was, like, three feet away." She grinned and shrugged as they approached her easel. "So, we're here."

"Well, thanks for the tour." Remi grinned. "Would you mind some company while you do your thing?"

"I don't know," Julianne teased. "The element of surprise has really become the hallmark of hanging out with you. I don't know if I could do without it."

As she was finishing her sentence, Remi turned and started walking away. "Hey! Where are you going?" Julianne called to his back. Just as suddenly as he'd walked away, Remi turned around and strolled over to Julianne's easel.

"Fancy meeting you here," Remi started again, feigning shock. "Do you come here often?" He arched his eyebrows, clearly amused with himself.

Julianne met his line and raised him a cliché. "Sure, I come here all the time, just hoping to run into someone tall, dark, and clumsy."

"Run into, eh? Didn't your sister say the same thing the other night?" Remi cocked his head toward her and squinted, as if hoping she wouldn't vanish into thin air if he blinked. Julianne knew that look—she was wearing the same one.

"Probably. It's the Kahn sense of humor. Gives us away every time. I think it's the by-product of seventeen years spent in a very small space together—eventually we'll turn into the same person. Me, my dad, and Chloe will all morph into one huge Mega-Kahn." She absent-mindedly picked at the stickers covering her water bottle, peeling the edges away so that the Nalgene logo was visible for the first time in several summers.

"Sort of like Transformers?" Remi grinned, his big eyes fixed right on her.

"Oh, totally," Julianne continued. "But none of that turning-into-a-big-robot crap. We'd have really practical powers. Like the ability to obliterate an entire gallon of ice cream in a single sitting. Or to steal the arts section out of the Sunday paper with lightning speed. Additional arms for the pottery wheel so we could make multiple vases at once. You know, the basics." She giggled. She'd almost peeled a border all the way around her Decemberists sticker.

"I won't lie, that's pretty sweet. If my family had crazy powers we'd probably just sort our laundry into whites and darks telekinetically. Or teleport ourselves back to work from the dinner table to get a few more hours in."

"Nothing like really utilitarian powers, I guess." Jules unscrewed the cap of her Nalgene and took a huge gulp before offering it to Remi.

He shook his head, but his eyes lingered on the spot on the rim of the water bottle where Jules's lips had just been. "I mean, it's not as boring as it sounds," Remi continued. "My family's actually really great. We're just not that, um, original. We're more *Leave It to Beaver*, I guess. You know?"

Julianne didn't really know what he meant, and said so. "Not really, now that you mention it. My family's always had a sort of free-form, go-with-the-flow way of approaching everything." Even Chloe's compulsive volunteering and studying were organic; they were things she did because they made her feel alive. Jules tilted her head toward Remi thoughtfully. "I can't really imagine a family being structured any other way. My family's a little bit 'follow your bliss,' if you know what I mean. As long as Chloe and I are doing the best we can and doing it for the right reasons, our dad is pretty much happy with whatever."

"What does your mom think about that?" Remi looked at her as if she were describing a totally different world.

Julianne paused, setting her water bottle down at the base of her easel. "Not much. She's actually dead."

Remi's jaw dropped like someone had released a little lever inside of his face. "I'm . . . I'm . . . sorry," he stammered.

Jules wiped a bead of sweat from in between her blue eyes and shrugged. "Don't worry about it. Sorry to be so blunt, but you didn't say anything wrong."

Remi reached out and touched her wrist, then sheepishly shoved his hands into his back pockets.

"So, what are you doing on this beach?" Julianne asked, feeling a familiar blush starting to creep up her neck. "I mean, other than looking for more innocent victims to terrorize with your demolition derby moves?"

"I think you're safe for now—there isn't a keg in sight." Remi laughed a deep, rich laugh. "I was surfing with some guys I met down at the boardwalk earlier, and then I was just exploring the beach, really. You saw my brief attempt at a second run in the water. I haven't been in town long; I don't know where anything is, but I really love this beach. What are you doing down here?" He laughed again, gesturing at Julianne's easel. "I mean, obviously I know what you're doing right now. But what's your usual beach routine?"

"I live down there." Julianne gestured vaguely over her shoulder, toward her family's small cottage. "But I come here to paint. I'm starting my summer job next week, so I won't have access to afternoon painting light much longer."

"Can I see what you're working on? Or are you one of those super-secretive artists?" Remi asked with a sly wink.

"Oh, super-secretive. Definitely. That's why I would never in a million years work in the middle of a public beach where everyone could see me." Julianne laughed. She took Remi's hand and led him back around the easel, where her landscape was still sitting deserted and unfinished.

Remi was silent for a minute, looking at the easel and squinting his eyes. He even crouched down to take in Julianne's painting from a different angle. Then he took a few steps back and squinted at it again.

"It's not anywhere near finished," Jules started. "I'm having a lot of trouble with the light. The highlights on the water, especially. I don't know what my problem is; I'm usually not this—"

Remi cut her off midsentence. "This is good. Like, really good. Julianne, you're *really* good." He crossed his arms over his chest, impressed, and stepped back to view the painting again from a distance. Julianne noticed that for a skinny guy, he was in no way lacking in muscle definition. She felt a little bit embarrassed at her blatant check-out but, really, that's what he got for standing there and being so unapologetically attractive.

"I bet you say that to all the girls . . ." She smirked, her eyebrows arched.

"Not *all* the girls." His eyes twinkled as he countered her teasing. He walked back around the easel and plopped down in the sand, staring at the waves in front of him. "So, will you tell me about it?"

Julianne walked over and slid down in the sand next to him, hugging her knees to her chest. "Tell you about what? How good I am? I mean, clearly I'm fantastic." She rolled her eyes playfully.

"Well, duh," Remi replied, a smile creeping across his face. "And I'd love to hear about just how much you completely rock some other time. Maybe over coffee or something? But I was actually referring to your painting."

"Oh." Julianne's breath leaked out of her slowly. She was sitting barefoot on her beautiful beach, splattered in paint, with a gorgeous guy who genuinely wanted to talk about her work. And she was ninety-eight point nine percent sure that he had just asked her out. She took a deep breath and started to talk about her painting.

"So, you know I told you about my mom?" Remi

cocked his head and nodded. "Well, she was an artist. A really incredible artist. She showed her work all over the country—and in pretty much every gallery in Southern California. She also lectured at all these different universities and illustrated all of my dad's children's books. There was really nothing she couldn't do. When she first got sick, she still went outside and painted every single day. I mean, *every* day. But when she died, there were six paintings she never had a chance to finish. I've finished up three of them—I made two of them into multimedia things, that's more my style. That and photography. But this one I'm trying to re-create as if she'd had the chance to finish it. Her paint, her light, the whole nine." Julianne felt herself getting antsy—she had a hard time sitting still when she was talking about her mom—so she circled back around the easel and walked a few feet down the beach, picking up seashell fragments. "One of the other pictures is this really bright portrait of our house in November. The light is really ethereal and the beach is all vacant—it's really cool. So I expanded it on a larger canvas and intercut some of my photography, prints, and etchings with it."

"Wow. What are you doing with the other one?" Remi asked.

"It's hard to explain," Julianne started. "But I guess you could say I sort of rebuilt it." She described how she had sliced it up into strips and installed it, strip by strip, into a huge wood-and-wire sculpture. The whole piece was huge—she had constructed most of it standing on a step stool smack in the middle—and Julianne loved the feeling that she could live inside of it. Both had won regional art shows in their respective years. The portrait of their little beach cottage was even on display in the lobby of the Chamber of Commerce.

"Wow." Remi looked at Jules with pure astonishment. "That's amazing. You and your mom must have been close."

"Very. Our whole family is." She stared ahead at the ocean.

"So, is that why you're an artist? Because that's what she did?" Remi leaned in, scooting a little closer to Julianne.

"Nope," she said thoughtfully. "I mean, not really. I'm an artist because I can't *not* be. It's like breathing, you know? I've been doing this since I was too young to understand that it was what Mom did. But I guess she's become a part of it. Knowing it's something we share, even if she's not here anymore. Continuing her legacy, or whatever."

"But you don't want it to be all about the loss," Remi said softly.

"Yeah, exactly." She stared at him, hard, her blue eyes locking with his big brown ones. "That's exactly what I was going to say."

Remi leaned in toward her and draped his arm across her shoulders. Julianne leaned into his side and breathed him in, surprised at how natural and easy it felt.

Suddenly, fat raindrops splattered everywhere, shooting down in rapid fire. Julianne and Remi propelled themselves up from the damp sand and ran around trying to collect Julianne's things. Julianne quickly found her flip-flops and slid them on, then hurried over to pack up her palette and brushes. Remi had already disassembled the easel and was lifting her canvas gingerly off the sand. "You know what?" Jules began, an idea forming in her brain.

"Hmm?" Remi asked, still packing up.

"This looks like it'll blow over in a few minutes. Let's just toss a cover over the painting and wait it out. We'll be fine," she suggested.

Remi grabbed a tarp from Julianne's art supply stash and covered her painting gently before sliding back down beside her in the sand.

They sat side by side and took in the sights of the beach in the rain. When she squinted, Julianne could just make out her house in the distance. Even dwarfed by the huge glass-and-metal McMansion that had sprung up next door, Jules thought her house was beautiful. Even from down the beach it looked warm and cozy—small, but completely charming. She silently fumed looking at her new neighbors' pretentious monster home, but then she took a deep breath and decided to let it go. She turned to Remi and said brightly, "You know what? I feel the rain letting up. I think I'm going to start setting my stuff up again. I'll be able to do some really neat stuff with the light after the rain clears out."

Remi nodded and smiled, obviously impressed with Julianne's dedication. "Since I took all of your stuff down, I think it's only fair that I help set it back up. Sound like a deal?"

"Deal," Julianne said, grinning back at him.

They got up from the sand and walked in small circles, gathering Jules's discarded art supplies, just chatting. As he turned and checked out the full panoramic view of the area, Remi's face lit up. "Oh—I totally know where I am!" *Great,* Jules thought. *If Remi is figuring out his way around already, he'll definitely be able to find his way back!* The tiny hairs on her arm prickled at the realization that her hand was nestled in his. Standing on this familiar stretch of sand with Remi, the beach looked more gorgeous than ever. Just as Jules had predicted, the rain was weakening, the clouds brightening and clearing. By the time Jules and Remi had reassembled her work spot, the afternoon storm had all but cleared up. Surveying the horizon, Jules noticed that most of the surfers hadn't even come off the water when the rain started.

As Julianne removed the tarp from her painting, Remi plunked down on the sand next to her, his surfboard sitting by his side like a loyal dog. Jules eased down into the sand beside him and he scooted just a millimeter closer. They were near enough that she could practically feel the tiny goose bumps dotting his arms. She was tempted to rest her head on his shoulder and re-create the cozy scene that had been interrupted by the rain a few minutes earlier, but Remi beat her to it, wrapping his arm around her shoulders. Julianne was shocked and giddy—it was like he could read her mind. The heat of his body touching hers seemed to electrify the air, and Jules half expected the wooden legs of her easel to go up in flames.

"So, you surf?" she asked, breaking the silence with a question she could have answered herself.

Remi laughed. "No. Not at all. I just carry around this surfboard to impress the ladies. It was pretty awkward in Seattle, but I think it could work magic down here. What do you think?" he joked.

"Oh, yeah," Jules replied, looking from the surfboard to Remi's bathing-suit-clad body. "Definite chick magnet."

"How about you?" Remi asked, turning his head toward Julianne. "You're a California girl. Do you surf?"

"I'm okay," Julianne admitted, shrugging, "but not great. My best friend, Kat, is a fierce surfer, though." Her blue eyes sparkled wickedly as her gaze locked with Remi's. "Maybe you could show me a few moves? Help improve my game?"

Remi took his arm down from around Julianne's shoulders and gestured toward his board. "Have time for a lesson?"

Julianne felt the tiniest bit shy as she peeled off her tank top and lay down on Remi's board. "Okay!" she called over her shoulder. "Surf school is now in session."

Crouching next to her, Remi laughed. "So, show me how you usually paddle out."

Julianne windmilled her arms above her head, imitating her freestyle stroke. She could feel the muscles of her back moving as she fake-paddled, and she couldn't help but laugh. She also couldn't ignore the irony of Remi, who was new in town and from a city basically devoid of ocean and sunshine, giving her pointers on surfing. Not that Julianne minded. Sneaking a glance at Remi, who was paying complete and total attention to each movement of her arms, Julianne didn't mind one bit.

"Good," Remi instructed. "Now, push up!"

Julianne tucked her arms back within the perimeter of the board and, in one strong, fluid motion, used them to lift herself off of her stomach and onto her feet. Once she was up, she readjusted her bandana, put her hands on her hips jauntily, and turned to Remi. "How am I doing, Coach?"

"Your form's pretty good," Remi answered earnestly, standing up. "I think you might want to use your upper arms a little more when you're pushing up, though. It'll give you more momentum. Can I show you?"

"Sure. Do you want to demonstrate, or . . ." Julianne trailed off.

"Nope. Get back down on the board, and I'll show you, as you're doing it. That way you can feel it while it's happening," Remi suggested.

Giggling silently, she hopped back down onto her stomach, already giddy with anticipation. She situated herself on her stomach in the middle of the board. Remi leaned across her, and Jules shivered slightly, both from his shadow creeping across her back and from the proximity of his body to hers.

"Okay, now move your arms in like you're going to push up," Remi instructed. As Julianne began drawing her arms inward, she felt his hands on her shoulders. She was momentarily afraid that her arms would give out under her, and she'd belly flop on the surfboard. Talk about embarrassing! "Now," Remi coached, his hands never leaving her shoulders, "move your arms a little bit farther apart, and try pushing up again."

As Julianne prepared for her second try, she heard a series of quick beeps, and Remi's hand suddenly flew off her shoulders.

"Crap!" Remi muttered. Julianne rolled over and looked up at him.

"Sorry," he explained sheepishly. "The alarm on my

cell went off. I'm supposed to be home for dinner with my folks in ten minutes. I guess I, um, lost track of time."

"Then I guess I should get off of your surfboard," Julianne suggested regretfully. Why did it feel like they were always interrupted before the best part?

"In a minute," Remi agreed, sliding down next to her. He lifted one hand to Julianne's cheek and wiped away some sand. "But not quite yet." He leaned in and softly planted another mind-numbing kiss on Julianne's lips. Jules felt her pulse quicken as she kissed him back. This was *definitely* the best part.

Reluctantly, Remi pulled his lips away. "Um, I guess I should be getting home."

Now it was Julianne's turn to act on instinct. "In a minute," she said. She scrambled up off the surfboard and dashed over to her abandoned easel. She grabbed one of her tiny paintbrushes and dunked the end in blue oil paint. "So it might be possible that I, maybe, lost your phone number on the beach the other night." Julianne approached Remi with the paintbrush. "Maybe. A little bit."

"Oh, really," Remi said, feigning offense.

"And it's definitely possible that I don't want to make the same mistake twice," Jules continued. She reached over and took Remi's arm by the wrist, turning it so the underside of his forearm was facing up. "So this time, I'm giving you *my* number." Julianne took the paintbrush and jotted her phone number in blue oil paint along the inside of Remi's arm.

"That tickles," he protested halfheartedly.

"Yup," Julianne responded in mock-seriousness. "I know. And it will until it dries. So the tickling will remind you to put my number in your phone."

"Very clever." Remi laughed. "I love a girl with fore-sight." He leaned in and gave her a soft peck on the cheek, as if to illustrate his point. Julianne sucked in her breath involuntarily. Even his kisses on the cheek made her shiver.

"So I guess you'd better head home, huh?" Julianne asked.

"Guess so. And I guess you'd better get back to painting before you lose the light?" he replied.

"Guess so," she answered, even though she'd forgotten about the painting entirely. "Call me sometime?" she asked, half teasingly.

"Absolutely." Remi smiled. "If for no other reason than because I don't have any turpentine in the house—your number will probably be on my arm for the rest of the summer," he joked, picking up his surfboard.

"That's what I like to hear." Jules grinned back. "Enjoy dinner."

"Thanks! See you later." Remi smiled at her one last time before turning and jogging back up the beach.

Julianne wiped sand off her arms and turned back

toward her easel, determined to keep her cool and not check Remi out as he jogged away. She picked up her paintbrush and got exactly two strokes onto the canvas before she just couldn't resist. Trying to be as subtle as possible, she turned slowly and looked for him on the horizon.

She spotted his lanky figure several hundred yards in the distance. Her eyes locked on to him just in time to see him place his surfboard gently on the ground, dust himself off, and walk right through the giant glass door of the Moores' giant glass house.

Chapter Four

✦

Several hours later, Julianne was still in shock. Every part of her churned in confusion, even as she tried to focus her attention on hanging out with Chloe. She'd thought that some quality sister-time would be just the thing to help her get it together.

"I mean, he's still pretty perfect, though," Julianne mused out loud. "Isn't he?"

Chloe swept her hair off of her shoulders into a high ponytail and then adjusted the drawstring on her pink-and-yellow-striped lounge pants. "All I know is that we're never going to a party where they only have PBR ever again," she mused. "Think about it—crappy beer, crappy guys. They go hand in hand. From now on it's good drinks or bust."

"Things went that well with Michael, huh?" Julianne chucked a pillow at her sister.

"Like I said, crappy beer, crappy guys. He seemed like such a sweetheart in physics lab."

Julianne picked at the spots of dried paint still clinging to her hands as she considered her response. "Well, you know, clearly it's time to start paying less attention to physics and more attention to chemistry."

"Oh Lord, Jules. Stick with art, okay? Because comedy? Not your thing." Chloe tried to look miffed, but her hazel eyes were laughing.

"When did it start going downhill?" Julianne flopped onto her back and stared up at the floral border edging its way across the top of Chloe's bedroom walls.

"Oh, I don't know . . . about half a second after he told me that I was pretty good at physics 'for a chick.'" Chloe's heart-shaped face screwed up into a horrified grimace. "I'd say it was a pretty quick descent to rock bottom from there."

"No way!" Julianne squealed, popping bolt upright again. "There's no way—he couldn't have actually said that!" She tossed another one of Chloe's smooshy throw pillows at her sister for emphasis. "Wait, did he actually say that?"

"How could I possibly make this up?" Chloe lobbed the pillow back at Julianne's head. "What part of 'arrogant jerk' isn't coming across clearly here?" She paused and gnawed her left thumbnail thoughtfully while Julianne continued to stare, wide-eyed. "Good thing he's not a communications major, I guess," she said, sighing finally.

"You mean, because he should really never talk to anyone ever again?" Julianne asked, laughing, before taking a swig of water. "I mean, honestly—ew!"

"Julessssssss!" Chloe wailed. "Why is every guy I meet a complete loser? Are there no guys on the entire West Coast who aren't completely sketchy? And *you*—" She turned her attentions toward Julianne. "You cannot even think about things going any further with Remi!"

"But . . ." Julianne snapped open her mouth in protest. "He's . . ."

"I know, I know." Chloe cut her off decisively. "He's smart, he's hot, he's funny, blah blah blah. So are lots of other guys. But you know what he's got that other guys don't? Parents who are trying to bulldoze our beach. I wouldn't mess with that, Jules. Crazy runs in families."

"Not everything runs in families, Chloe. Dad has green eyes, and neither of us do. It doesn't necessarily mean anything, right? Besides, if you'd seen him this afternoon . . . oh my God. He completely got everything I was saying about painting. And his surfing lesson was pretty much the hottest thing *ever*. And—"

"Okay, points duly noted." Chloe was all business. "So you'll have some awesome memories. But you can't keep seeing him. There's no way it can go anywhere good."

"But why not?" Julianne pressed.

"Because he's one of them, Jules. He's a McMansion Moore. His parents are terrors. They are the living embodiment of bad news." Chloe was on a roll. "And that house! Can you honestly imagine someone living in that glass house who *isn't* a complete and total jerk?"

"He's not a jerk," Julianne said quietly, feeling both absolutely certain of it and utterly confused.

"Maybe not *yet*. And maybe he won't turn out to be as complete a jerk as his parents, but still, nothing good can possibly come of dating him. The Moores are nothing but trouble."

"Can we please change the subject?" Julianne pleaded, her head swimming.

"Yeah, of course." Chloe's tone was bright again and Julianne felt herself relax instantly. "But promise me you'll think about it, okay?"

"Sure. Of course. Seriously, don't worry about it," Julianne assured both her sister and herself. "We have the entire summer to meet guys who don't completely suck. Forget guys, even. I have an awesome job working for Bill's crew. You're going to be over at the children's hospital—surrounded by hot med students, might I add—and it's going to be perfect beach weather for the next three months."

"That's more like it, except for the forgetting-guys part. Summer is totally a time of infinite possibilities. We'll work hard; then we'll beach harder. There is no room in that schedule for wasting time on two-faced boys who are tacky enough to hit on us after we've sustained minor head trauma." Chloe's voice was resolute. "So, what exactly are you doing for Bill this summer anyway?"

Julianne scrunched up her nose, thinking. "You know, I'm not entirely sure. He's going to give me a whole orientation on my first day. It's this cutting-edge house, though. I think I'm going to be doing some of the more creative touches. I know Mitch and Hunter work for Bill, but I think I'm going to be the only girl on the crew."

"That's the kind of detail I was looking for! That's what we should be focusing on! Forget *construction*. You're doing your art stuff, and that's cool, but it's the abundance of guys that's key in this scenario," Chloe cut in excitedly. She smirked. "I mean, of course, I don't care if you're working with truckloads of guys with serious manual-labor muscles," she intoned in mock-seriousness. "It'll just be nice to have some contacts if, you know, we need a handyman or two." She grinned mischievously and cast her eyes down toward the carpet.

Julianne smiled and shook her head. "Enough about my summer plans. Speaking of too much to do this summer, where does your final tally stand at the moment?"

Julianne watched her sister count off her obligations silently before answering. "Okay. I'm working at the children's hospital. Then I'm tutoring two afternoons a week and giving surf lessons on Saturdays. And I still haven't decided if I'm going to jump in for pickup volleyball. I want to have some time just to read and hang out on the beach."

Julianne smiled at her sister. Chloe was such an overachiever, yet she always found time to have fun in the midst of all her other commitments.

"I can't wait to go out with my camera and spend an entire day just hanging out by the ocean," Julianne gushed, visions of sunshine and brand-new surfer boys with guitars and dreadlocks already elbowing their way into her thoughts.

"And you know," Julianne added, "any poor decisions we make while on the beach can *totally* be blamed on our surroundings. I mean, if, for example, I happened to go for le petit joyride in the Moores' shiny yellow backhoe and their tacky glass house happened to get a little bit broken, clearly I could not be held accountable. It's that tricky beach terrain. No traction whatsoever." A devious grin spread slowly across Julianne's face. She twisted one long brown curl around her finger, relishing her own half-serious troublemaking.

"Ugh, there you go talking about *backhoes*," Chloe grumbled. "Don't get all *Ty Pennington* on me. If you're going to talk construction, can we at least talk about what you're wearing for your first day of work? The outfit is key, you know." Chloe leapt off the bed and bounded toward her walk-in closet.

Julianne looked at her sister. Chloe's warm face was frozen in determination. "You're totally right. A girl's gotta have her priorities straight. And clearly my fashion sense isn't focused at the moment. Style me. I am turning myself wholly over to your vision for my first day of work."

"Pinky swear?" Chloe's almond-shaped eyes looked even larger than usual.

Chloe extended the pinky finger of her right hand to her younger sister, who entwined it with her own. They both leaned in and shook on it.

"Pinky swear." Julianne shook a second time for emphasis. "But nothing white. And no blazers. Blazers are your thing. And also, if we could keep the UCLA paraphernalia to a minimum . . ."

Chloe and Julianne both looked at each other and stifled a giggle. Chloe stepped into her closet and tossed out a dozen items for her sister to try on. Pastel colors and scoop necks were flying fast and furious, and Jules had to cover her head to avoid being beaned by the better part of the Marc by Marc Jacobs summer collection. "Try those. All of those. Then we'll reconvene for a final decision tomorrow night. Now that that's taken care of . . ." Chloe trailed off.

"On to the next matter of business," Julianne finished.

"Popcorn?" Chloe was halfway out the door and darting in the direction of the kitchen.

"Popcorn," Julianne concurred.

"Chick flick?" Chloe called behind her.

"Chick flick," Julianne called back. "Just give me one second!" She ran over to her computer and typed out a quick email to Kat.

> *K–*
>
> *Do you think summer love is too good to be true? Ran into the guy from the party last night on the beach today and he's beyond amazing. We had an awesome conversation about painting and everything just felt so right. He gave me some surfing pointers. Maybe I'll be able to hold my own with you in the waves by the time you get home. One *major* catch, though—I think he lives next door. You know, in the monster house! What do you think that means? I'm so confused! Help!*
>
> *In other news, work starts tomorrow. I'm excited. How are your classes? Any cute Madrid boys? Send me pictures already!*
>
> *xoxo*
>
> *–J*

Chapter Five

✦

Julianne's curly hair spilled out of her bike helmet and trailed behind her in the warm breeze. As she pedaled her blue beach cruiser down familiar Palisades roads, she was thrilled that the environmentally conscious philosophy of her "green" summer job had inspired her to bike to work. Seeing familiar faces and gorgeous scenery on her twenty-minute bike commute put Jules in a fabulous mood before the day had even really started.

As she pulled up in front of the construction site, hopped off, and locked up her bike, Julianne spotted a half-dozen workers already hanging out, drinking coffee, and looking at blueprints. Solar panels, wood beams, and a ton of different kinds of tile were scattered everywhere. The outline of the house that was already standing was boxy and sleek—modern without being obnoxious. After a few quick hellos, she set out pacing around the skeleton of the house. She was unbelievably excited to help design the rest of the project. Not only was it great from an artistic standpoint, but Bill had explained in his last e-mail that everything about the project was eco-friendly. Green building materials, green power, clean design. It was going to be a totally cutting-edge house, giving as much back to the neighborhood as it took in the building. *This project,* Julianne thought, *is going to completely and totally rock my world.*

She meandered from room to room, making sure she knew where everything was before she got to work. Wending her way through the maze of beams and dry-wall, Julianne walked smack into Mitch.

"Jules, hey!" His greeting jarred her into focus.

"Oh, hi, Mitch. How's it going?" Julianne smiled and gave her cross-country teammate the once-over. So far, the job had been good to him. Sweat slicked his muscles, and his face had the glow of someone who'd spent a good amount of time outside. "Lookin' good."

"Thanks," he replied. "You look . . ." He paused, seemingly surprised at the words that were coming out of his mouth. "Great. Really great." He caught himself. "Um, I mean, it looks like you're having a really great summer." His cheeks flushed slightly. Julianne made a mental note to thank Chloe for insisting that she wear a pair of gray Roxy shorts and fitted green American Apparel T-shirt with her Timberland work boots.

"Okay, people!" Bill was waving them over to the front of the house.

Julianne and Mitch shuffled back to the group of workers, Jules saying hi to a few guys she recognized from her interview with Bill a few weeks earlier. A few of them, decked out in their cargo shorts, tool belts, and T-shirts looked at Julianne with widened eyes, but mainly they nodded their heads in acknowledgment.

"Okay. First things first," Bill started back up again. "Jules, you already know Mitch?" Julianne and Mitch both nodded. "Great," Bill said, adjusting his tool belt. "Then if there's anything you need, you can just ask Mitch. I'm sure he'll be happy to take care of you. Anyway," Bill continued, "are you ready to jump into the wonderful world of bathrooms?"

"Excuse me?" Julianne asked, laughing. She plunged her hands into the pockets of her shorts and leaned back a little, waiting for Bill to clarify.

Bill smiled and explained. "The owners of this place want to see some pattern options for their bathroom tile before we start laying anything down. How would you feel about sketching some designs for them to choose from?"

Julianne beamed, thrilled to have an artistic project

to work on already. "That sounds fine," she said, trying not to gush.

"Good. After Mitch introduces you to the rest of the guys," Bill concluded, "you can head into the trailer. I've got you all set up." He smiled and walked off.

Mitch and Julianne made their way through the site, greeting the other members of the crew. "That's Jack." Mitch pointed across the yard to a burly college guy wearing a Lakers cap and a sleeveless T-shirt. Julianne recognized him from last summer, when he had bussed tables at the Fishtail, but Mitch told her that he had also competed in the lumberjack games for three years running and was a silver-medal holder in log rolling. Tom was on the baseball team at Stanford (and, Julianne noticed, had the arm muscles to prove it). Beau was an English major at UCLA. Nick, who was Julianne and Mitch's age, was just in town for the summer visiting his aunt and uncle; he was a snowboard pro up in Utah, where he'd be returning at the end of the summer.

Jules tried to keep her mind from wandering during the introductions, but she couldn't stop thinking about the lines of the house, the angles, and there was a Lily Allen song playing on repeat in her head. *"Sun is in the sky, oh why oh why would I want to be anywhere else?"* She was still humming to herself and bobbing her head softly when she heard Mitch saying her name.

"Jules? Julianne? Earth to Julianne?"

"Oops. Sorry." Julianne blushed. "I was just thinking about my first project."

"Yeah, sure." Mitch smirked. "You're surrounded by college guys and you're busy thinking about bathroom tiles. I buy that."

"Hey, I'm a much better multi-tasker than you give me credit for." Jules laughed, punching him lightly on the upper arm.

"I'm sure you are. C'mon, let's head over to the trailer." He pointed and led the way.

"Thanks for the tour, Mitch. Let the guys know that it was *great* meeting them, okay?" she joked, winking.

"Later, Jules." Mitch laughed.

Julianne walked up the steps of the trailer and knocked three times. When there was no response, she propped open the door and walked in. Then she spotted a note on one of the empty desks.

> *Julianne,*
> *Unfortunately we don't have a desk for you, so you'll sort of be drawing wherever you can find space. The desk I'm setting you up with to start is the new project manager's, but I'm sure he won't mind if you borrow it for the day. He seems like a nice guy. Give a holler if you need anything.*
> *Bill*

Alone in the trailer, Julianne stretched out, twirling her pencil between her fingers. She propped her legs up on the project manager's desk, like the queen of the site. This was definitely going to be a fun job. She tapped the eraser of her pencil on the vast expanse of white space on her blank page. A fresh sketchbook was one of her favorite things in the universe—so full of possibility. Still tapping her eraser against the page, she began to brainstorm about tile designs. Since it was an eco-friendly project, maybe something with leaves? Or maybe something geometric to match the lines of the house? Or something with an ocean motif, since they were so close to the beach? Dividing her paper into four quarters, she decided to give each idea a chance and then commit to fully sketching the best two designs for the owners to choose from.

Julianne was in the middle of her second sketch when the door creaked its way open. "Hello?" she called out, not looking up from her drawing. She was in the middle of sketching a line of mosaic tiles curling into the branches of a larger tile tree.

A familiar voice answered, "I didn't know this office came with a chair warmer. Man, this job gets better every day."

Julianne looked up from her sketch. Her stomach did a series of quick backflips when she saw the new project manager beaming at her.

"Remi?" she said, dropping her pencil onto her—correction—*his* desk.

"We've got to stop meeting this way." He laughed. His laugh was even deeper and richer than Julianne remembered, and his face was warm and bright.

Julianne swallowed hard. How could this be happening? She felt like she had somehow fallen out of her life and landed in a romantic comedy. If she just counted slowly to five, maybe Drew Barrymore would walk in and the transformation would be complete. Remi was completely decked out in preppy professional attire, but his hair was still adorably shaggy and ruffled from the breeze. He was wearing gray dress pants, shiny square-toed shoes, and a light blue button-down with the sleeves rolled up for that "casual yet approachable boss" look. Remi's outfit amused Julianne. Even though his tie was clearly expensive, it was adorned with tiny T-squares. She wasn't sure whether to laugh or groan—it looked like his mother had dressed him. Still, it was impossible to ignore how hot he looked. Remi wore his authority well, and the little trailer was suddenly filled with his friendly confidence.

Smiling back without even realizing it, Julianne took another deep breath and said simply, "Hey."

Chapter Six

✦

Julianne felt like there wasn't a single part of her that wasn't shaking. She was being torn in a million directions from the inside out. She wanted to be mad—furious even—that Remi was here. Where did he get off interfering with her totally eco-conscious summer job, especially considering what his parents were doing? Still, whether he was the spawn of the devil or not, there was no denying that he looked like the same cute, charming Remi she'd spent the day with on the beach. Worn out from her internal debate, Julianne settled on total shock, took a deep breath, and swung her boots down off his desk. *This will be fine,* she told herself. *This will all be okay. I'll just focus on what I'm doing and soon I won't even notice he's here.*

She pushed her dark curls back off of her face and gathered up her sketchbook and pencils. Squinting out the window at the crew working outside, Julianne thought about making a quick getaway before he could reach her, before realizing that the only ways out of the trailer were over Remi, under Remi, or through him. There were no two ways about it; he was standing directly in front of her. She opened her mouth to speak, but Remi beat her to it.

"I wasn't expecting to see you here. It's a nice surprise," he said with a coy smile.

"Yeah, this is unexpected," Julianne managed in response. Unexpected? That was the understatement of the year.

"I guess we never had the 'how are you spending your summer vacation' talk, did we?" Remi chuckled. "During the school year, I intern for this architectural firm up in Seattle. They do a lot of really interesting stuff—eco-friendly, sustainable—and a lot of structurally innovative stuff, too." Remi spoke quickly, with what seemed like genuine enthusiasm.

Jules couldn't help notice the way his button-down shirt drew attention to his strong chin and the way his eyes sparkled when he spoke. *No, no, no*, she reminded herself. *You can't like him. You just can't.*

Julianne could tell that he was really excited about the house they were building, maybe even as excited as she was, but she was determined to affect a look of casual disinterest. So what if he was cute, smart, funny, and came complete with cool academic interests? He was probably still a jerk. Well, he was certainly the *son* of jerks. And there was a good chance he would turn into a jerk himself. He probably wasn't even that interested in eco-design anyway—maybe he had been wait-listed for some suit-required corporate internship and had gotten shuffled into this job.

"So when my folks told me they were moving down here, it seemed like a really good opportunity to check out the LA office," Remi added. "It's a newer office, a little bit smaller; so that's how I got to project manage this summer. Basically, it's a cool job and an independent study all rolled up into one, you know?" Julianne nodded slowly, only half-processing what he was saying. "So what are you doing here?" Remi asked. Julianne tried to avoid his eyes, which were still—much as she hated to admit it—warm and syrupy.

"Bill Cullen, the contractor, set me up with the job," Julianne explained. "He saw one of my sculpture pieces in the Chamber of Commerce and called and asked if I'd be interested in trying this. Plus, I like to be outside, work with my hands, and try new things. Like you said, it's sort of a combination of business and pleasure." The moment the words were out of her mouth, Julianne kicked herself. *Business and pleasure?* she repeated to herself. *Did I really just say that out loud?*

Remi nodded appreciatively, oblivious to Julianne's discomfort. He wiped his hands on the sides of his pants before responding. "I want you to know, I can be totally professional. I promise not to make this weird."

Julianne's blue eyes widened with disbelief and her jaw muscles tightened.

"Excuse me?" she managed to choke out, trying desperately to figure out how things could possibly get any weirder. She pushed up the sleeves of her T-shirt, like she was getting ready for a fight. The whole construction site, which had felt so magical and full of possibility just half an hour ago, seemed to be shrinking, closing in on her.

"I said that I want you to know that I can be totally professional," Remi repeated sweetly. "And that I promise not to make this weird."

Julianne's head was swimming. She couldn't believe he was here at this construction site, when his parents were clearly the antithesis of everything the eco-house represented. Even more, she couldn't believe the effect he was having on her. This was never going to work. It was too confusing, too messy. But she wasn't about to walk away from this fabulous job without a fight. That would mean leaving the crew short a person *and* relegating herself to a summer spent indoors selling surf wax or ice cream.

"Julianne? Are you okay?" Remi asked gently, peering

at her across the desk.

Please let him disappear, please let him magically disappear, Julianne silently begged. She squeezed her eyes shut tight, but when she opened them back up, Remi was still there. And looking at him made her weak in the knees.

"I think you should leave," she blurted out. "Or I should leave. Someone should leave."

Remi's eyes widened in surprise. "Um, okay. I can go back outside, but it would help if you could tell me why I'm going?" He said it like Julianne had presented him with a riddle and, if he solved it, there'd be some sort of prize.

"I believe in what everyone's doing here, and I want to be a part of it," she said shakily.

"Okay," Remi said again slowly. "So far, it sounds like we're both on the same page."

"I don't think we are," Julianne said, more definitively than she felt. "At least, I know I'm not on the same page as your parents."

"What?" Remi crinkled his brow, genuinely befuddled. "What do my parents have to do with this job? You don't even know my parents."

"Why didn't you tell me that you're Remi *Moore*?" Julianne shot at him, eyes blazing. Her voice was a lethal combination of pure sugar and pure steel.

"Why didn't I tell you my last name?" Remi tried to keep up with Julianne, but he looked like a lost puppy.

Julianne tried not to get distracted by how adorable he was when he was confused. *Just stay angry,* she told herself. *Now we're getting somewhere.*

"I didn't realize I hadn't told you my last name. I guess it never came up. I can try again. Hi, I'm Remi Moore. Nice to meet you." Remi smiled at Julianne, waiting for her response.

Julianne just shook her head from side to side, mute.

"Okay," Remi said, trying again. "Remi is short for Remington, but no one other than my folks ever uses the full name. My full, full name is Remington Justin Moore. When I was in third grade the other kids teased me because they thought Remington sounded like the name of a British butler. My cousin Sophie also said that the Remington is a type of razor or something, but I'd never heard of it." He continued to smile weakly in Julianne's direction. When Julianne still didn't answer, his face slumped a little. "Jules," he said quietly, his big brown eyes begging. "I really don't understand. What's wrong?"

Her frustration boiling inside, Julianne finally spat out, "Your parents' house! That's what's wrong!"

Remi looked at her as though she were arguing her case in ancient Mayan or something. "Why do you care about my parents' house? I really don't understand."

"It's destroying the beach!" Julianne nearly wailed. "You know, the beach where I grew up? Where I live now? With my family? The beach where we hung out the other day?"

"Julianne, this doesn't make any sense," Remi protested. "Listen, I'm really sorry that you don't like the house, but it's my parents' house. Not mine. I didn't design it. I didn't build it. And, last time I checked, my parents weren't in the habit of asking the professional opinion of their eighteen-year-old son before making major life choices. If they were, I wouldn't have spent my entire life toting around the name Remington. If you're wondering, I also didn't get to weigh in on their retirement plans." He paused, as if waiting for Julianne to crack a smile.

"You just don't understand," Julianne replied bitterly. "Do you even know what that house could do to my family?"

"No!" Remi exclaimed, his face knitted in frustration. "That's what I'm trying to say—I have no idea! And I have no idea what I have to do with any of it. Please, please explain it to me!"

Julianne's mind raced. *Was he playing dumb? How could he not see? It was so obvious!* Overwhelmed with emotion, she plopped back down in the desk chair. As she opened her mouth to try to explain one last time, the trailer door opened and Mitch popped in.

"Hey, Jules." He nodded his head in acknowledgment at Remi before continuing. "Just wanted to check in. How's it going? Need anything?"

Julianne thought for a split second before getting up and gathering her things. "Yeah, Mitch, actually I do. Can you please tell Bill I'll be working on my sketches from home this afternoon? I just don't feel right about hogging our project manager's desk any longer than absolutely necessary."

"Yeah, no problem. Everything okay?" Mitch tilted his head and looked at her curiously.

"Yup. Absolutely fine." Julianne nodded. Brushing past Remi and Mitch, she dashed out of the trailer as quickly as humanly possible. She couldn't wait to get home.

Chapter Seven

✦

Julianne was exhausted beyond belief when she got home half an hour later. Her confrontation with Remi, followed by the threat of nasty drivers cutting her bike off, had left her wanting to do nothing more than curl up in her bed with a sketchbook, e-mail Kat, and then call it a night—even though it was only three in the afternoon. She turned her key in the door and had barely placed one foot on the doormat when she heard spastic panting coming from the next room. It sounded like someone had let a hyperactive puppy in from the sun. Before Jules had a chance to think about it, Chloe ran into the hallway—her hand clapped over her mouth—doing measured breathing exercises to avoid hyperventilating. Julianne hadn't seen her sister this worked up about something since her college acceptance letters showed up a week late. Normally Chloe was calm, upbeat, and cheerful. Standing in front of her right now, though, was a trembling mess who just happened to be wearing Chloe's straight-legged, dark-wash Joe's jeans and fitted pink blazer.

"Chloe, what's wrong? What's going on?" Julianne felt her own heart race as she stared at her shaking sister. "Is it Dad? Is Dad okay?"

Chloe nodded and pulled Julianne by the wrist over to the beach-facing bay windows in the family room. A few hundred feet down the beach, Julianne could see what was inhibiting Chloe's breathing. While Julianne was at work, the Moores had set up huge orange fences all the way down the beach. Every five feet a hazard sign hung off the fences shouting PRIVATE PROPERTY: ALL TRESPASSERS WILL BE PROSECUTED.

Jules couldn't believe it—just when she'd thought things couldn't get any worse! She stood with Chloe at the window, rubbing her sister's back and muttering, "Those rats, those little rats. Those complete and total dirtbags."

Chloe, whose breathing was finally slowing to normal, managed to squeak out, "What? Who?"

"The Moores, who else?" Julianne practically spat the name out. The orange gates looked offensive and menacing, even against the baby blue afternoon sky. It was like they were living in a biohazard zone or a bombed-out shell of a city. The gates themselves were aggressively orange—like they were there specifically to tell every other part of the color wheel to go to hell.

Their father, who had been working down the hall in his studio, ambled into the room.

"Girls, what's going on in here?" He stopped short when he saw their eyes fixed on the orange fences. "Oh, yeah, that."

"Had you already seen this?" Chloe yelped. Their father was always mellow, but they expected more of a reaction when their home had just been surrounded by what appeared to be giant, Day-Glo riot gear. "Why didn't you say anything?"

"It's not worth discussing," Dad replied, turning from the window. "It's just a show. It's just supposed to scare people away. If they were really planning on doing something, they wouldn't need to make such a big spectacle about it. They'd just do it." Chloe and Julianne both nodded. It might have been cold comfort, but he definitely had a point. "Don't worry, girls. It's going to be fine. We'll figure something out." He sounded so certain, so sincere, that Julianne couldn't help but relax a bit.

"Okay, I need to shower. I'm covered in dust from work. But I think I'll go for a quick run first." Jules turned toward the stairs. She got as far as the doorway before the vision of the glaring orange gates compelled her to spin around toward the window for one last look. Dad was sitting on the window seat, his face tilted slightly away from the beach view, his fingertips lightly touching the glass. For the first time, Julianne saw something behind his eyes that hadn't been there before. For all of his mild-mannered, easygoing confidence, their father was scared.

✦ ✦ ✦

After her run, Julianne took the steps two by two on her way back to her room. Her sneakers were still caked with a little bit of sand, but, for the first time all day, her head was clear. She held on to the banister outside of Chloe's room, stretching her calves and quads, and listened to the ebb and flow of her sister's voice as she chatted on the phone. She was obviously catching up with one of her Kappa Delta sisters, so Jules decided to leave her be until after she'd showered.

Twenty minutes later, Kelly Clarkson was blasting from Chloe's Bose iPod dock and the girls were shouting along at the top of their lungs. "Since you been gone, I can breathe for the first time . . ." Chloe was up on the bed in full-on rock-star air-guitar mode, her hair flying wildly around her, while Julianne was sprawled out on her back on the floor, her bare feet propped up on

Chloe's bed. When the song ended, Chloe flopped down on the bed, laughing, and straightened her flowered pajama bottoms and shell-pink tank top.

"Why do I love that song so much?" she asked Julianne. "It's already a few years old."

"Yeah, but it's definitely a classic." Jules laughed. "Which must be why they still play it on the radio, like, constantly."

Chloe shrugged. "I told Dad we'd handle dinner tonight. What are you in the mood for? Fish? Pasta? Or maybe just a big salad?"

Julianne really wasn't sure what she wanted. Not in terms of dinner, not in terms of anything. Her fabulous summer job was going to be tainted with special guest appearances by Remi Moore. Her special tribute painting to her mom was getting more difficult by the day. And the construction and the gates on the beach certainly weren't helping anything. Her photography was better than ever this summer, but nothing she did made her painting seem any more polished. Julianne pulled her feet off of Chloe's bed and tugged her body up from the floor. "Do you mind if I check MySpace?" she asked. "Kat promised she'd post some pictures of Madrid."

"Sure, it's on," Chloe tossed back. "Just make sure I'm logged out."

Julianne sat down in Chloe's gigantic rolling chair and piloted it into the computer cove of Chloe's white wicker desk. She ran her fingers over the touch mouse to turn off the screen saver (a rotating photo slide show of Chloe with her sorority sisters, Chloe with her premed friends, Chloe volunteering, and Chloe crossing a bunch of 5k finish lines. Damn—her sister's life looked exhausting!) and logged into MySpace—her current go-to method of procrastination.

Julianne looked at the familiar blue banner spread across the top of the screen and checked her "bulletin space" for news from her friends who were away for the summer. She tried to ignore her disappointment that Kat's photos still weren't up, and she skipped over to her own photo collection. Mitch had taken a picture of her in a hard hat this morning and promised he would post it.

"Whatcha' looking at?" Chloe asked, coming up behind her sister to peek at the screen.

"Not much," Julianne said, flipping through her photo album at a rapid pace. She wasn't really amused by MySpace at the moment.

"Ooh, I like that one," Chloe piped up, pointing to a picture of Julianne sitting on a cooler at a beach bonfire. Her hair was blowing everywhere in the beach breeze, and her face was lit orange by the fire.

"Hey!" Chloe smacked Julianne on the shoulder in excitement.

"Hey what?" Julianne asked, rubbing her shoulder.

"Let's look up your new favorite project manager!"

Chloe laughed, putting quotes around "project manager" and deepening her voice.

"Ew! No!" Jules squealed, giggling. "I am adopting a strict 'no bringing work home with me' policy from here on out."

"Oh, c'mon!" Chloe wheedled, using the camp counselor voice that suckered Julianne in each and every time.

Jules folded. "Okay, you do it though. It's your idea." Julianne got up and surrendered the cushy rolling chair to its rightful owner. Chloe slid into the computer corner and pulled her laptop closer to her. She selected search and typed in "Remi Moore." Julianne tried to contain her nervous laughter.

"Jackpot!" Chloe burst out. "There are seven pages of Remi Moores. There are literally dozens of them. Who knew so many people shared such a weird name? Let's put our detective hats on. If I were an obnoxious project-managing, land-destroying hipster, where would I be?" Julianne laughed as they started clicking.

About six pages in, Chloe stopped clicking and excitedly poked Julianne. "Found him! This is so totally him!" Julianne leaned down and squinted at the computer, momentarily wishing that she wore glasses.

"What does his headline say?" Julianne asked.

"Pompous land-hog seeking non-sustainable relationship," Chloe answered.

"Wait, *really*?" Julianne whipped her head around and

squinted at the screen. As much as she wanted to dislike Remi, that didn't seem right at all.

"No, of course not," Chloe fessed up. "But I think it would be much more apropos than 'He who awaits much can expect little.'"

"Is that actually his quote?" Jules asked, her eyes wide with disbelief.

"Mmm-hmm," Chloe confirmed.

"That's Gabriel García Márquez. I love that quote," Jules murmured, impressed. Why did he have to be so smart? Couldn't he just be the weaselly jerk Chloe thought he was? It would be so much easier.

"Well, unfortunately, there's no rule that great authors are the exclusive domain of those who don't suck, so I guess he's entitled." Chloe yawned, lazily twirling her hair with one hand as she clicked around the rest of Remi's profile. "Oh, check out his pictures! This is hilarious!" Chloe had flipped right to a picture of Remi in costume for some sort of campus party at UW—dressed as the Mona Lisa.

"Well, with the wig . . . and when he tilts his head that way . . . I guess I can see the resemblance." Julianne laughed. Although she didn't want to admit it, she was amused by Remi's costume, even more than she was amused by what an awkward-looking woman he made. They flipped through his other photos: Remi and his friends after a tug-of-war. Julianne had to pinch herself to stop from swooning at how cute he looked in his sweat-soaked T-shirt with mud-streaked cheeks. Remi and his dad at the top of a mountain. Remi at a microphone, sound-checking for someone's band. Julianne's heart caught in her throat when they flipped to a picture of Remi with his arm around a pretty redhead in front of the Space Needle. Then she caught the caption: "Sophie visits Seattle. How many Moores can one city handle?" Ah. Sophie *Moore*—a cousin, perhaps? Julianne was a little taken aback by how hard she'd been hit by jealousy before she read the fine print. She reminded herself to play it cool—maybe she'd find something in the profile that would prove once and for all that he was actually a bad guy. But as Chloe clicked through, picture after picture registered for her as neutral to positive. Finally they came back to Remi in his Mona Lisa getup.

"Never in my life have I seen someone look that much *worse* as a drag queen!" Chloe howled with laughter. "Let's see—what else can we find out about Mr. Moore here?"

Jules read from the screen "Status: single. Here for: networking, friends. Hometown: Seattle. School: University of Washington."

"C'mon, get to the good stuff!" Chloe urged.

Julianne might have felt the slightest pang of anticipation. "Okay, okay, here goes. General interests: architecture, music, movies, building things, politics, soccer, surfing, screen-printing band T-shirts, guitar, hiking.

Music: the Killers, the Gossip, Mates of State, Sufjan Stevens, Common, Mos Def, Sinister Urge." Julianne had to hand it to the guy—pompous jerk or not, he had pretty awesome taste. His hobbies, his favorite music, his favorite books, they were all really cool. *Stop it,* she reminded herself. *That's not the point.* "Heroes: Frank Lloyd Wright, Olmsted, Gandhi, my dad."

"Wow, so he's totally got a hero-worship situation with his dad, huh?" Chloe asked.

"Maybe he's like a little dad-bot—a clone or something!" Julianne laughed, happy to find something to criticize. Even as she said it, though, she felt a smidge of guilt. She knew what it was like to feel that way about a parent—even if she'd never admit it publicly.

"Hey, Jules, how's this for a crazy idea," Chloe began thoughtfully, as she got up from the rolling chair. She steered Jules toward the chair by her shoulders and, once Julianne had plunked herself down, swiveled the chair back toward the monitor.

"Uh-huh," Julianne responded, enjoying the change of view but not quite sure what Chloe was thinking.

"You should stalk him!" Chloe said brightly.

"Um, Chloe, hate to break it to you, but that's exactly what we're doing right now. We're total stalkers," Julianne reminded her with a laugh.

"Hold on—let's think about this," Chloe suggested. "What if you really did it?"

"What? Stalk him?" Julianne was incredulous.

"Not like actual stalking—no restraining orders required or anything. Maybe 'spying' or 'personal information recon' is more like it. You know, like, 'know thy enemy'?"

"Something about that just doesn't feel okay to me," Julianne countered hesitantly.

"Jules, you're going to spend all day with him, all summer. In an environment where talking about building is the norm. Aren't you the least little bit curious to find out what else the Moores plan on conquering? With the surveyors and the gates? What better place for someone to casually mention his or her home improvement plans than at a contractor's site? They're never going to be up-front with Dad—it would take away all of their bargaining ability. It's the best way to stay a step ahead," Chloe pressed.

"You know what? I think you might just be on to something," Jules conceded slowly. "Going incognito, playing innocent. By day, I'm a mild-mannered designer-slash-construction worker, but by night, I'm an undercover super-spy for the Kahn compound, acquiring top-secret information in the service of protecting all that's good, beautiful, and righteous against the evil forces of the Moore empire!" *Plus,* she thought, *it would be nice to have another reason to talk to him at work.*

Chloe grinned slyly. "Now you're talking!"

Chapter Eight

◆

Julianne spent the next three weeks at work in an eco-friendly nightmare. Every time she turned around, Remi was standing over her shoulder. He was settling comfortably into his role as "boss," and while he was always a kind, encouraging, and respectful equal to the other guys on the site, Julianne felt like he was there for the sole purpose of making her life more difficult.

She was cutting boards at the circular saw the first time it happened. She had pulled her hair down from its ponytail to put on her safety goggles, so it hung loosely down around her tan shoulders. She eyeballed the length of a board and drew a crisp pencil line across the two-by-four before arranging it on the circular saw.

She was about to rev up the saw when she heard *his* voice over her right shoulder.

"Um, Julianne, can I have a word with you?" Remi's voice was quiet.

Julianne spun around, trying to keep her face neutral. "Sure thing, but it needs to be quick. I don't want to get behind on these boards."

"That's actually the thing," Remi responded. His voice was gentle but Julianne could have sworn he was savoring every word. "I think it would be better if you laid off the circular saw for a while."

"Why? What are you talking about?" Julianne's cheeks stung with embarrassment at the implied demotion. She used power tools all the time with her sculptures. The last installation she'd made was the size of a tree house, and she'd assembled it out of all sorts of boards and planks.

"It's not so much your craftsmanship that's the issue. It's more about the dress code." He sounded concerned, almost parental. Jules, however, had a sneaking suspicion that he was embarrassed.

Julianne looked down at her denim cutoffs, her black ribbed tank top, and her worn-in Pumas. All over the site, guys were wearing practically the same thing, with a few tank top and sneaker variations. She ran her fingers over her belt, which was made of elaborately braided nautical rope. "Is this the problem? I mean, I can take it off." She began to tug at her belt buckle.

Remi's face went bright red at the suggestion of Julianne unbuckling. "N-n-no," he stammered. "That's not it. It's your hair. You can't have your hair hanging down like that when you're standing over the circular saw. You could get pulled in. It's a liability. It's, um, on all the safety code posters, and I know it seems like a really nit-picky thing, but these tools are really dangerous so . . ." His words tumbled out in one rambling run-on sentence.

"Are you kidding me? I only had it down for a second—I was just pulling on my goggles." Julianne was almost too shocked to be angry.

"Look, all I know is I turned around and you were standing over the platform marking your board and your hair was hanging on the circular saw. If you want the whole DIY haircut look, you can use the scissors in the office during lunch." His attempt at a joke flew right over Julianne's head. "For today, how about you measure the boards, but let Jeremy cut them?" Remi mumbled, darting his eyes toward the floor as he gestured to a new guy—a junior water polo player from Julianne's school, who had joined the crew the day before. "He's only here for the week, and it'll be really good experience for him," Remi finished quickly. Julianne nodded, too stunned to argue. "Hey, Jeremy!" Remi called. "Come over here! Jules could use a hand."

As Jeremy sauntered over, it only took a second for Jules to understand why the entire girls' volleyball team was always gathered around his locker. Unfortunately, it only took two more seconds for Jeremy to prove that he was also a tremendous jerk. "C'mon, baby," he said purposefully to Jules. "Let a real man show you how it's done."

Julianne fumed. How dare he act like the problem here was that she was a girl? Maybe there *were* bigger losers than Remi on this site, after all.

"Sorry, Jeremy. Remi wasn't able to find a real man, so you're going to have to help me instead," she shot back. "But if a real man comes by, feel free to take notes."

Undeterred, Jeremy tossed his arm around Julianne's shoulders to guide her, barely avoiding wiping out on the laces of his untied Nikes. They made it almost all the way back to the circular saw before Julianne whipped around and mouthed, "I'm going to get you!" at Remi's receding back. She couldn't help but notice that he'd finally started wearing better pants—they hung loosely over his long legs—but she tried her best to ignore the improvement and focused on her anger.

"Damn it," Julianne muttered to herself, her ocean blue eyes brimming with hot tears. Between kicking herself for not being more cautious about her hair and feeling the weight of Jeremy's toned, chauvinistic arm around her, she didn't know what to be humiliated about first.

From that point on, it seemed like everything that

could go wrong did. Julianne spent three miserable days filing and photocopying invoices in the site trailer. The inside of the trailer was covered in fourteen distinct shades of beige and one very distinct odor of mildew. She spent every cooped-up moment in there dreaming of the murals she'd paint on its crumbling rent-a-walls if only she had access to the crew's paints. Even on the days that she was in the trailer choosing colors, designing lighting, or planning the landscaping for the owners, she resented the trailer just for *being* there.

Even worse, Remi was everywhere Julianne turned. She felt like he was looking over her shoulder, just waiting for her to mess up. Of course, she found herself making stupid mistakes when he was around. She could almost forgive him for keeping such a close watch on her, but she wasn't sure she could forgive herself for letting him psych her out so much. If she started to drill a board into place without sanding the rough patches down first, she'd turn around and, sure enough, Remi would be standing right there. Accidentally attach a solar panel upside down? Remi suddenly appeared two feet away, and Julianne could swear his eyebrows were arched.

The more Julianne stressed out about Remi's suffocating proximity, the closer he seemed to get. She felt paranoid, anticipating that he would find fault even with her best work.

"Hey, Julianne—that panel could be a little bit

straighter, okay?" she muttered to herself, mocking his helpful suggestions.

Not even five minutes later, his imagined voice popped back into her head with "Hey, Julianne—that tile could be set a little bit closer to the others, okay?"

"Definitely. I'm on it," she responded to herself, even managing a jaunty salute. She was totally losing it.

Half an hour later, when she saw Beau's broad figure lumbering across the site, she tensed up immediately: "Hey, Julianne—you might want to think about using a different bit on that drill, okay?"

"Anything you say, chief." Julianne sighed. She was getting exhausted just thinking about it.

"Hey, no need to get snippy with me," Beau said, raising his hands in faux surrender. "I just don't want to see you get showered with splinters is all."

"You don't want to see me get all splinter-y—or you were *sent* over here to tell me I'm doing something wrong?" Julianne asked suspiciously, fiddling with the Velcro on her work gloves.

"Whoa . . ." Beau said, laughing, arms still up in mock defensiveness. "I'm here with only the purest of intentions. No nefarious plotting whatsoever. And every time I've talked to you in the past week—if you don't mind my saying, Jules—you've asked me if Remi sent me over. A few too many unnecessary protests, if you know what I mean."

"Hey now, Mr. Big Imagination," Julianne protested,

half-laughing. "I think you're spending too many of your lunch breaks reading romance novels—don't think I haven't seen you huddled back by the trailer—it's starting to go to your head!"

"Maybe," Beau replied slyly. "Or maybe not all the sparks flying on this site are from your drill bit . . ."

"Oh, *shut up!*" Julianne said, laughing as she rolled her eyes. Beau shrugged and headed back over to his workbench. "Drama queens," she muttered to herself. "Guys are such drama queens."

By the end of the third week, Julianne had resorted to singing to herself—or rather, to every song on her iPod playlist—to keep herself calm and focused on work rather than on Remi. When that lost its charm, she moved on to imagining elaborate spy scenarios. Her favorite one involved her and Chloe—decked out in matching James Bond spygirl outfits—rappelling into the Moores' mansion under cover of darkness only to find out that the whole thing was an elaborate cover for an international drug cartel. They called in the FBI and not only were the Moores sent to a remote island to grow bananas and repay their debt to society, but the girls were both rewarded with presidential medals and the deed to the entire beach. Which they, of course, designated as a free public space and artists' colony. Julianne played this fantasy over and over in her head until she began to feel a little bit creepy for wishing it were actually true.

When she wasn't imagining new and creative ways for the universe to karma-smack Remi and his family, Julianne waited with her ears perked for any mention of Remi's name around the site. Whenever one of the other guys mentioned Remi, Julianne would hang back pretending to tie her shoe, or take additional measurements on something she'd just measured twice a few minutes earlier. Unfortunately, they never seemed to say anything, except what a great guy and good manager he was.

She was becoming a pro at looking casually disinterested or distracted while secretly absorbing every last syllable being uttered around her. In short, she was well on her way to being the best spy in Southern California. Okay, maybe not. But definitely the best spy in the Palisades.

Chapter Nine

✦

Julianne crept around the corner, trying to stay crouched down low to escape notice. She was holding a small, electronic stud-finder in her hand, working her way around the perimeter of the wall. If anyone walked by, it would look like she was checking to see where to attach the moldings at the bottom of each wall. She kept her head down, waiting to make her move. Only a fellow spy would have recognized that Julianne was honing her skills—waiting for Remi to come around the corner after his 10 a.m. meeting. James Bond had nothing on her.

After three weeks of progressively more intense surveillance—of what she and Chloe were now jokingly calling "the subject"—Julianne had come up with precious little that was of any help to her cause. She had, however, developed a whole arsenal of easily deployed spy tricks. The stud-finder was her latest innovation. As Julianne knelt on the floor, she was torn between feeling incredibly clever and beyond sketchy. On one hand, she was undercover—complete with techno-props. On the other hand, she *was* sort of curled into a ball as an elaborate excuse to try to overhear a few seconds of Remi's morning plans.

She heard footsteps coming and snapped back into her position—her face shielded, the stud-finder level with the floor and beeping softly. The click-click-thump of shoes was getting closer, and Julianne strained to hear what was being said. After a few more moments, she began to get worried. Nonetheless, she kept her head down and the stud-finder level. Five minutes passed, then five more. Julianne's hands were beginning to cramp up around the stud-finder, and she couldn't feel her right knee after sitting on it for so long. Finally, her patience was rewarded with a snippet of conversation.

"Dad, I know it's important . . . of course I do. Yeah, Dad, I know. I understand I have a responsibility. Yes, for the fourteenth time, I promise I will not forget." Remi's tone was a blend of stress and annoyance, and Julianne could picture him pulling at the tie around his neck as he walked. "Yes, Dad, I know I'm too old for you to be keeping tabs on these sorts of things for me. I promise you, I can handle it myself."

Julianne's ears were burning from the strain of listening in on the conversation. As Remi walked past her along the other side of the wall, she inched slowly in his direction. What could Remi and Mr. Moore be discussing? What was so crucial that only Remi could attend to it? Maybe his dad had him gathering land value information from Bill or from Dawson and Dawson. Or maybe they were going to be expanding the perimeter of their property again and Remi was going to set up the gates. Julianne practically fell over herself to hear Remi's last words before he turned the next corner into the space beyond her earshot.

"Look, Dad, I have something I need to get to in my office. I know there are other things you want to discuss, but can we just do it later? Yeah, I'll be around." Julianne heard Remi's cell phone click shut before he'd even spat out "Goodbye." As his footsteps faded in the distance, Julianne refused to be deterred. After waiting a few minutes to be sure he'd left the house, she popped her head up to see whether the coast was clear. No one on the left; no one on the right. Julianne crouched like a sprinter waiting at the starting block and, after a second's hesitation, dashed out toward the trailer, stud-finder still in hand.

She tiptoed around the back of the site trailer, being

careful not to step in any of the patches of dry, brown summer grass around the perimeter, just in case they made a crunching sound and gave away her where-abouts. She knelt down in the space under the trailer's back window, steadying herself with one hand on the grass and one on the plastic siding of the trailer. It was like waiting with the stud-finder all over again, only now her spy prop just looked silly. She waited and waited to overhear even a hint of conversation coming from Remi's desk, but he wasn't talking and her calves were screaming from her awkward crouch.

Patience frayed, Julianne hopped up onto her tiptoes and peered in the back window of the trailer, careful to keep her head down and her mane of curly hair—always a dead giveaway if someone was trying to spot her from a distance—out of sight. From her new vantage point, Julianne found she was able to hear much more clearly than when she had been hunched behind the trailer. She could hear the drip stop of the coffee pot by the desk and the whir of the photocopier in its power-save mode. Then she heard a squealing sound from inside the trailer. *Squealing tires are secret-agent pay dirt,* she thought. Shifting to get a better view, Jules was just able to make out the trailer's bathroom door opening. Her mind worked hurriedly to figure out what sneaky, no-good things Remi was up to in the trailer bathroom, but before she was able to formulate any sort of convincing hypothesis, the door slid all the way open and Remi appeared in her line of vision. Wearing nothing but a towel.

Jules felt her eyes grow wide as her gaze followed Remi's body across the trailer. Hanging around the construction site had been kind to him; his muscles were smooth and well defined. Even the farmer tan from his rolled-up work shirt sleeves showcased how strong and tight his arms were. Julianne had always thought that "rippling muscles" was just a figure of speech, but as Remi made his way across the room she had to admit that his muscles were, in fact, rippling. A few stray drops of water from the shower lingered on his chest, clinging stubbornly, until one by one they slid way down to six-pack abs, tracing a trail down his stomach, then finally disappearing into the towel.

As Julianne peeped through the window, trying to control her breathing, she heard a series of mechanical knocks on the door of the trailer. It sounded like someone was banging a cookie sheet with a baseball bat, and the noise was just enough to startle Jules into ducking her head out of view. Huddling against the back of the trailer, she heard the clomping of business shoes on the front steps. Julianne pressed her ear against the wall.

"Remington, I presume this isn't what passes for business casual on a site these days." Julianne heard a sharp baritone scolding Remi. She couldn't imagine anything more humiliating than one of his bosses from Dawson and Dawson popping by to check on the project site and, instead, finding him half-naked. She felt a pang of sympathy for him.

"Dad?" Remi gulped. "What are you doing here?" Julianne felt as shocked as Remi sounded—she never would have guessed that the voice belonged to Remi's father. He sounded so cold and businesslike.

"I think a better question, young man, might be what are *you* doing? Last time I checked, pants were still required at work," Barton Moore countered. *Ouch*, thought Jules. *He clearly just took a shower. His hair's still wet!*

"Would you believe an unfortunate drywall accident?" Remi asked gamely.

"Not particularly," his father barked back.

"Well, that's a shame. Because that's exactly what happened. I was completely covered with powder and I figured it was better to clean up and change now, rather than walk around all day looking like I'd been caught in a freak snowstorm." Julianne heard Remi trying to be his casual self, but she also heard the tension in his explanation.

"Remington, that's a pathetic excuse," Mr. Moore responded icily. Julianne held her breath, waiting for Remi's response. She couldn't help but feel that Mr. Moore was being unduly harsh—it wasn't like he'd walked in and found Remi playing Wii on the job. He was cleaning up after a work accident and heading back to his crew. Clearly there was some precedent for this sort of thing; why else would these trailers include showers in their bathrooms?

"I'm sorry you feel that way, sir," Remi replied. Julianne felt herself soften, detecting the tiny tremble in his voice.

"Listen, Remington," Mr. Moore continued. "It's about time you grew up and learned to handle responsibility. How am I going to trust you to take over *my* business when you can't stay on top of one project crew?"

"But—" Remi began to protest.

"But nothing." His father charged on. "Are you on the site supervising your crew, or are you hiding in this trailer like some spoiled celebrity?"

Julianne gasped at Mr. Moore's nastiness and clapped her hand over her open mouth. She hoped that the sound was muffled by the wall of the trailer. She felt the sting of recognition as Mr. Moore continued to lay into Remi—after all of her faux pas on the site over the past few weeks, she knew all too well what it felt like to get called out for an innocent mistake.

"You can't expect your crew to respect you," Mr. Moore concluded solemnly, "until you give them a reason. I challenge you to earn their respect, Remington. And mine."

"Yes, sir," Remi answered. Julianne was shocked that Remi wasn't fighting back—anyone could see how well-respected he was around the site. Guys two and three times his age, who had been in this business longer than Julianne had been alive, asked Remi's opinion on pretty much everything. The newbies looked up to him as an authority. Hell, she'd hoped against hope that he would just disappear into thin air, but even Julianne had to respect the job Remi did. He was *that* good. And, what's more, Julianne noted in spite of herself, he did it all without ever tearing any of the other guys down or trying to make them feel small—which was more than she could say for his father.

Julianne felt the little hairs on the back of her neck prickle and stand up as an uncomfortable thought worked its way into her brain. Maybe Remi really *didn't* have anything to do with the construction of his parents' McMansion. Mr. Moore seemed sort of . . . tyrannical. It was impossible for Julianne to imagine him asking anyone's input, especially someone he treated the way she'd just heard him treat Remi. Clearly, she had some more detective work to do.

✦ ✦ ✦

When Julianne got home from work that evening, the house was empty. Dad was at his monthly meeting of local children's book authors, and Chloe had left a note saying that she'd be home from the hospital around ten o'clock.

Julianne tossed her things onto the living room sofa and headed upstairs to her room. When she logged on to her Gmail account, she saw one new message. She hoped it would be a long, newsy update from Kat in Spain, but instead the message was from Chloe, reading simply, "How did it go?" Julianne moved the message into her trash folder and turned on her Internet browser. After a few minutes of distracting herself with home-made bags, prints, and jewelry at etsy.com, Julianne logged on to MySpace. Before she knew it, she was back at Remi's profile, combing it for clues.

As Julianne embarked upon her first solo MySpace "recon" of "the subject," she got a little twisting feeling in her stomach. Was she taking this too far? The guy on this MySpace page wasn't some sort of teenage Donald Trump. MySpace Remi listened to good music, and read good books, and had lots of funny friends who wrote clever comments about the time he'd been in an ostrich race or the time he'd built an exact replica of someone out of toothpicks.

Consciously, Julianne knew that she needed to do whatever she could to take the fuel out of the Moores' assault against her family and their beach. But the tiniest of tiny pangs at the bottom of her gut kept complicating things. Julianne was so surprised by her own inkling of a thought that she swatted at her head to chase it away. She knew what side she was on. She needed to do what was right for her family, and nothing was going to get in her way. She logged out of MySpace quickly. But, before she could clear her head, she clicked into Google and entered the search term "Barton Moore."

Chapter Ten

◆

Julianne was close to discovering the perfect color of blue. She was covered from head to toe in various shades of blue oil paint—battle scars from struggling to finish her mom's painting. As she swirled her brush on the palette, she felt the tension and frustration of the past few weeks begin to melt away. She traced circles in the sand at her feet with her big toe while she mixed her paint and hummed to herself. Her oversize sunglasses were perched on top of her head, and her hair was pulled back into two braids, all of her speckled with at least three different colors of blue.

She tried to shrug off the last few weeks of confusion. It was all she could do to keep focused at work with Remi around every corner. And, as every super spy knows, being undercover is exhausting. The hardest part for Julianne, though, was coming home and feeling like she wasn't able to snap out of her Remi-induced work-day funk. Every time she took out her mother's painting, something didn't feel quite right. The light was off, or her oils were too thick, or her brush strokes were too uneven. It was always something.

But today the light was perfect, and it was like Julianne had been given brand-new eyes to appreciate it with. She was mixing blue that was almost too vibrant to be real but was the *exact* color of the afternoon ocean. She cranked up her iPod and laughed at the absolute per-fection of it all. Keeping her eyes on her canvas she stood up and stretched her arms out to soak in the glorious day. Then a deafening noise erupted, making her wheel around, terrified that it might have been a car crash.

But the real cause of the ruckus was even worse.

Julianne stared down the beach toward the Moores' house. The confrontational-looking fencing erected around their sprawling property had multiplied and was now nearly blocking off all access to the beach. Behind them, a parade of huge shiny bulldozers and backhoes were lined up like enormous, angry hornets. One by one they rolled out and started leveling the entire area. Julianne felt like she was being punched in the stomach.

Leaving her things on the ground, she crept closer to the action, trying to put her newly acquired spy skills to good use. She turned off her iPod, leaving the earphones in, so that anyone who saw her would think she was just enjoying an afternoon on the beach—or what was left of the beach—with a sound track. Ducking down near the fencing behind one of the many towering dunes created by the bulldozers, Julianne was basically invisible to anyone in the area. She shivered as she curled up into herself, waiting to see what would happen next. She didn't have to wait long.

"Hey, guys! Coffee break?" A voice bellowed from the top of the dune. Julianne heard the echo of four keys turning off four ignitions, and then the clomping of eight individual work boots scampering down the beach toward whichever grunt had been sent on a Dunkin' Donuts run. (Okay, maybe she was projecting a *little* bit on the last part . . .)

"So, what's the game plan for the afternoon, Tom?" she heard a deep voice call out across the dune.

"More demolition. We need to clear this entire area. No brush left. It needs to be buildable ground," Deep Voice Number Two, presumably Tom, called back.

"How much ground are we talking here?" asked a third guy.

"The whole thing. We're taking out this entire pen." Tom didn't hesitate for a moment.

"What are they building?" Deep Voice Number One asked. "Pretty big demo order for a house."

"A gym, I think," Tom said offhandedly.

Julianne scanned the dunes around her and let her eyes rest on the ocean. It shimmered another new shade of turquoise in the afternoon light. She shuddered. How could anyone think that a gym, or a sauna, or any other extravagant convenience was more important than this beach? There were gyms all over. Already built and good enough for everyone else she knew.

"Like an LA/Sports Club?" joked another guy.

"Nah, not a franchise or anything." Tom laughed. "They're building a gym addition onto the house. A waterfront gym."

Julianne felt like she was going to burst out of her skin. A *gym*? The Moores were destroying this beautiful beach, taking land away from people who had loved it their entire lives, so that they could have a better view from their *elliptical machine*? Why couldn't they just put a couple of machines in their basement like normal people? Or work out on the actual beach? Maybe they should hire a live-in spin instructor too! Just when she thought there couldn't be a more stupid, ridiculous, petty reason for the Moores to keep building onto their monster mansion, they completely surprised her by raising the bar yet again. What could three people need so much space for? Two people, when Remi went back to school! Julianne was appalled.

She felt a burst of cold air as a new shadow fell over

her. She shivered and crossed her hands over her bare arms. Then the shadow cleared its throat. Julianne's eyes shot up in alarm. Remi was towering over her, his no-longer-so-skinny arms crossed in front of his chest, looking much more imposing than the twelve-foot dune.

"What are you doing here?" he demanded.

"Nothing. You know. Just listening to my iPod," Julianne said casually, trying to shrug while slowly standing up.

"I hear the sound quality's a lot better if you actually turn it on." He raised one eyebrow. Crap.

"Thanks for the hint. Now, if you don't mind, I'd like to be left alone." Julianne tried to capture her sassiest comeback voice.

"Left alone to do what? Continue eavesdropping on my father's construction crew?" There was self-righteousness rising in Remi's voice, mingling with teasing amusement. Julianne felt her pulse rising along with it.

"I think you mean demolition crew," Julianne corrected, matching him note for sarcastic note. "I don't see any construction going on here—just a whole lot of bulldozing. And I don't need to explain myself to you. Some parts of this beach are still public. At least for now."

"Julianne, what the hell is your problem?" Remi burst out, clearly frustrated. Julianne felt a pang, seeing Remi's usually handsome face contorted and shouting.

"This is my dad's dream house, and they're making great progress."

"Progress? This isn't progress! It's . . . it's . . . greedy and selfish. Your family is grabbing up every last morsel of space, every last grain of sand, so that you can have all of it to yourselves. It's not about making something—it's about proving that you're the biggest kid in the sandbox." After weeks of lying low and "monitoring progress," it felt so good to just yell and let her anger pour out.

"I don't understand why you're taking this so personally!" Remi bellowed back at her. "My dad is an amazing architect and this is his home. It's all he's ever wanted—it's his legacy. Why does that bother you so much?"

"You are defending *this*? What's with the infinite faith in your dad? How can you be so sure that he doesn't have it all wrong?" Julianne posed the question half as a challenge and half because she genuinely wanted to know.

"He's a brilliant architect!" Remi exclaimed, stretching his arm toward Julianne as if to put his hand over her shaking hands.

"And that means he can't be wrong? Why? He's wrong about you! He doesn't even think you can handle your own job site, but you trust him completely? That's just weird!" Julianne pressed on, undeterred by the fact that she had just inadvertently spilled the beans about eavesdropping earlier in the week.

"He's my dad, Jules. And he's worked his entire life for this," Remi said quietly, seeming to ignore Julianne's slipup.

"Well, did it ever occur to you that other people have worked *their* entire lives to afford the tiny slices of space that they live on? To sit at their windows and take in the view that you guys just bulldozed? The beach you're wiping out to make your gigantic glass jungle gym belongs to this entire neighborhood!" The words were tumbling out of Julianne's mouth, rolling over and over each other like marbles. Her mouth was thick with emotion and she was choking back tears. "Some people barely have *any*thing left, Remi," she wailed. "Do you really need to take the beach away from them for some house?" It was all Julianne could do to keep from sobbing. Her throat was burning from the screaming and from swallowing angry tears. She knew she probably wasn't making any sense, but she just needed him to hear her now.

"Maybe this is bigger than just 'some house'!" Remi shouted back at her. "My dad has been working for this for so long. I can't even tell you what it means to him—this is his artistic vision . . ." As he babbled on about his father's dream, his voice was so earnest that Julianne knew he meant every word. All he wanted was to make her understand.

But she couldn't stand it anymore. She had to cut

him off. If anyone needed to understand the *real* importance of this beach, it was the Moores. "Name one life that's being made more beautiful by what is happening here, Remi!" Her feet dug into the sand as she tore off down the beach to grab her easel. "Want to talk about artistic vision?" she cried, spinning back to Remi. "You know who had it? My mom! And her vision was all about this beach. The one your family is destroying! I can barely see her beach anymore. Soon it will be impossible to remember what she must have seen. But if you think I'm going to give up her beach without a fight, Remi Moore, you have another thing coming. This beach is more than just sand to my family—it's all we have left of my mother. It's the only place where she still feels alive. And I'm sorry if my family's past is getting in the way of your dad's bright, shiny future, but that's too damn bad!"

Out of the corner of her eye, Julianne saw Remi's mouth open to speak, his eyes wide. But there was nothing she wanted to hear from him right now. The sand flew up behind her as she raced to her easel.

Julianne's afternoon of perfect blue was perfectly ruined.

Chapter Eleven

✦

"Yo, Jules! Toss me those blueprints!" Beau called up to Julianne.

"No problem. Coming right down," she called back, tossing the rolled-up specs down from her perch in the rafters.

"Hey, J-dog, have you seen my tape measure?" asked Mitch from a ladder ten feet away.

"Have you tried checking your toolbox?" Julianne offered teasingly, flashing him her brightest smile. "Nine times out of ten, when you ask me for something, you already have it in there."

"That's our girl. Voice of practicality—what would we do without you?" asked Tom, covering for Mitch, who had turned crimson as he hurried down the ladder toward his toolbox. He'd been a little bit awkward all summer; ever since Julianne had appeared in her cute "first day of work" outfit. The other guys seemed evenly divided between ribbing him for his possible crush and hoping Jules would let him down easy. Everyone murmured in agreement, and Julianne thought for the millionth time how lucky she was to have this cool summer gig as den mother, little sister, and one of the guys. She felt like she was learning something new about the male mind every day.

Jules's typical morning banter with the boys was in full swing when Remi walked by, clipboard in hand. He made it almost past the group before calling back over his shoulder, "Julianne, if you have a second later, can you drop by the trailer? I have a question for you." The question was accompanied by low whistles from the other guys, but Remi never skipped a beat.

"Yeah, sure," Julianne called back to him, trying to sound equally nonchalant. "I'll come by as soon as I finish tiling upstairs." With that, she swung down from the beams and ran off to lose herself in tiling. She planned to throw herself into work in a blatant attempt to forget about her one-on-one with Remi.

✦ ✦ ✦

Julianne was enjoying the silence. For the first time in weeks, she didn't have a song, or a dashing spy scenario, or the remnants of a painful spat with Remi in her head. In what would be the master bathroom of Cullen Construction's very first eco-friendly home, it was just Julianne and the tile. Tiling, Julianne conceded to herself, was sort of like the paint-by-numbers version of mosaic. Sure, she was sitting in the middle of a big empty space with lots and lots of ceramic and a big bucket of cement, but focusing on the tile patterns was calming her down. Anything that could keep her mind off of Remi was all right by her.

Whenever she was alone in a huge room, Julianne liked to imagine herself transforming the entire space into art, just like Jean-Michel Basquiat, one of her favorite artists. Julianne caught her mind wandering and giggled to herself as she got back into the groove of her tiling. Apparently she couldn't turn her mind off after all.

Julianne was tiling diamond patterns into the floor, according to a diagram that Bill had based on Julianne's own design, when she heard a knock on the door frame. "C'mon in." She laughed absently. "The door's open!" In fact, the entire room was open—the walls had been framed but not yet filled in. She turned toward the door and felt her serenity evaporate as Remi approached, decked out in one of his weekday shirt-and-tie combos. *Whatever*, she chided herself. *At the end of the day, an attractive jerk is still a jerk.*

"Hey," Remi started.

"Hey," Julianne replied, utterly deadpan.

"Do you mind if I come in?" Remi hesitated before taking a step further into the doorway.

She wasn't in the mood for any sort of discussion right now. She just wanted to get back to her tiling. She tried to wave him away. "What, are you a vampire or something? You can't come in unless you're explicitly invited?"

Remi smiled faintly. "*Buffy* fan?"

Julianne looked him square in the eye. "Is there something you need?" She refused to get into a discussion about brilliant-but-cancelled TV shows with her former crush/current nemesis/boss.

"Can I talk to you about the other day?" Remi asked earnestly.

Julianne looked down at the flecks of cement covering her hands. "If you don't mind, I'd really rather not. I'm sort of in the middle of something. I'm sure your firm isn't contracting Bill to pay me fifteen dollars an hour to sit around and chat," she shot back brightly.

"Okay, let's try this again," Remi said, employing the same brand of persistence Chloe had used to rope Julianne into going to that fateful party in Malibu. "How about we talk about this job? If I'm not mistaken, Bill *is* paying you fifteen dollars an hour to consult with the project manager about the status of the project."

Julianne grimaced. "You know, Mr. Moore," she said sweetly, "I'm not sure how constructive that chat would be. I think you and I have very different goals for this project."

"Which are?" Remi's brow furrowed.

"Well, as I see it, your goals are more bottom-line related." Julianne continued to absentmindedly lay tile as she went on. "You ace this internship; you get a leg up on your architectural career. You get a leg up on your architectural career; you stand a chance of being the next big developer. You become the next big developer; you get to follow in your father's footsteps and, one day, you can make a big glass house of your very own, just like him." Julianne waited for Remi's rebuttal, but he was silent. His big brown eyes were trained on her hands as she continued to plunk down tile. "What's the matter? Did I hit too close to home?" she pushed on.

"Nope," Remi murmured quietly. "I was just wondering how someone could lay fourteen consecutive pieces of tile upside down without noticing." Jules felt her cheeks flush red. Why did she always make the silliest mistakes when Remi was around? "Do you need some help?" Remi offered.

"No, thanks," she replied tartly. "I've got it under control. I just need a little more space—you're making me feel claustrophobic, and it's hard for me to concentrate like this."

Remi pushed himself up from the floor and moved back about fifteen feet. "Okay, well that's something. So now that you've given your brilliant analysis of my reasons for taking this job, care to share yours?"

Julianne shrugged. She was hesitant to tell Remi anything even remotely personal. She'd been spying on him, trying to figure out what his motives were, for the past three weeks. Who was to say he wasn't trying the same tactic on her?

"I'm just going to sit here until you talk to me," Remi said. "So the sooner you spill, the sooner you can refocus on your tiles. How's that for motivation?"

Begrudgingly, Jules started talking. "If you must know . . ." She took a deep breath and then continued. "There are a few things that I really like. First, I get to spend my entire summer outside in the sunshine, instead of bagging groceries or folding jeans. Plus, for me, at least, a house is like a work of art. But on a grand scale. This bathroom is like a mosaic—only bigger. The whole frame of the house is one giant sculpture. It's beautiful, functional, oversize art. It's creative and it's fun. And I can't say I mind being the only girl on a crew of hot college guys, either." She looked up to see Remi staring right at her, his mouth open slightly, as if there were something he was trying to bring himself to articulate but couldn't. "Never mind." Julianne looked down at the tile again. "I certainly don't expect you to understand."

After a few seconds, Remi answered. "Why wouldn't

I understand? That's exactly how I feel about it, too. I mean, except for the part about the college guys. I want to make beautiful things. That's why I went into architecture."

Julianne stared across the tiles, avoiding looking up and seeing Remi's face. "You've got a strange way of doing it, you know?" She looked down at her hands. "Just following your dad's lead all the time . . ."

"There are a lot of different interpretations of beauty, Julianne," Remi said quietly.

Julianne's mind was tumbling over itself. Remi sounded sincere—more than that, he sounded like he *got it*. Like he knew about having a passion for something bigger than you. It wasn't the first time that he seemed to totally get it, either. She could feel his eyes fixed on her, and the back of her neck began to prick and blush. She shifted her weight so that she was sitting cross-legged on the half-tiled floor, and picked at stray threads poking out from the bottom of her shredding, knee-length cutoffs. She thought for a long minute before she spoke. "Okay, so tell me about it."

"About what? About houses? About art?" His dark eyebrows were pressed together and his forehead was lined in thought.

"About making beautiful things." She was challenging him. But she was also desperate to know. She leaned a little bit closer and tilted her long neck to look up at him.

"Okay, well . . ." Remi took a minute to get his footing before the words just started shooting out of him. "I love the idea that I'm making something permanent. I like seeing something I've designed or built and knowing that my hands made it." Julianne lifted her eyes just enough to see the earnest concentration on his face. "I like leaving a part of myself behind for people I may never even meet. Plus, I like using tools." He shrugged. "I guess that's it. I don't know."

Remi stared expectantly at Julianne, who raised her eyes until they met his. They sat on the tile floor, staring at each other, for probably two whole minutes in shocked, self-conscious silence.

Then Remi stood up quickly and walked out, leaving Julianne alone in the room with her upside-down tiles and a whole lot of messy thoughts.

✦ ✦ ✦

She floated through the rest of the day, replaying her interaction with Remi over and over in her head. Even if for just a split second, she'd felt a flash of whatever she had felt on the beach the night they first met—that kind of ease or understanding that had made her feel like she could talk to him forever. Julianne racked her brain while she set one tile down beside the next, over and over again. She swirled one finger around in the cement, watched the white goo harden on her skin. Remi had talked about architecture the same way she thought about art. But how could someone who felt something so pure about creating something new and exciting be so complacent about her naturally incredible beach—and the lives that people had built there? *"Deep down, Remi gets it. I may have been right about him after all,"* Julianne told herself, fixating on the flecks of light that had filtered in from the unsealed window frames in the bathroom.

✦ ✦ ✦

On her bike ride home, Julianne didn't put on her iPod or even notice the familiar Palisades faces that waved hello as she rode by. She was still too preoccupied with Remi and their cryptic conversation. Why should it even matter to her what his intentions were? No matter how good his ideas about art were, no matter how insightful he was, he was still the enemy. But he seemed to understand something that she'd never been able to articulate to anyone else. Jules tapped her fingers on the handlebars as she glided along, trying to puzzle it out. She wished her mom were here to help her make sense of the confusion. Her mother had always been so good at taking something and breaking it down into parts, turning it into something totally usable. Julianne had always assumed that was why she was such a good painter. She could isolate light, isolate space, isolate movement, polish them all, and then snap them back into place where they belonged. Jules had always been messier. She didn't re-create the things she saw around her; she broke them up and twisted them into new angles. Was that what she was doing with Remi—trying to make him into something else entirely because she wanted him to be something good? Her brain spinning and her stomach twisting, Julianne rode up to the house. She sat for a long moment staring up at her front door and wondered if it would be possible for her to ever find the middle ground, instead of the horizon.

Chapter Twelve

✦

Julianne climbed the stairs and walked directly past her bedroom, right into Chloe's. Flopping down on her sister's red flowered Marimekko comforter, she announced, "I give up!"

Chloe, who had been sitting at her desk filling out her daily log for her internship at the Children's Hospital, immediately snapped to attention. She popped out of her rolling chair and dove onto the bed, practically landing on top of Julianne.

"Tell me everything! What did he do? Oh, Jules, I knew he was bad news! So, what's the deal? Are they selling the property and moving to Iceland? They're not going to move out and sell it to some business, are they? That house is just ugly enough to have potential as a casino."

"No, it's not like that," Julianne hedged. "I had a lot of time to think about it at work today, and I feel like some pieces are starting to come together."

"What, what, what?" Chloe wheedled. "Is all of their building money embezzled? Can we call the IRS and shut them down? It's major, isn't it? I can just feel that it's major! Don't leave a sister hanging here!"

"I think we might be operating under slightly different definitions of 'major,' Chloe," Julianne prefaced, before switching gears altogether. "Oh, I don't even know. I had this really weird conversation with Remi at work today and now . . ." She paused, burying her head in a pillow. "I'm so confused!"

"What a jerk! Jules, you can't let him get to you." Chloe poked Julianne in the side playfully, but Julianne didn't even giggle. "C'mon, Debbie Downer—cheer up!" Chloe grabbed a throw pillow from the head of her bed and pressed it against her chest, like she was trying to squeeze answers out of the satin-covered down. "I'm sure there's a reasonable explanation for Remi giving you a hard time. Maybe he's an alien. No, wait; I've got it—they're plowing down the beach to make a puppy farm where they're actually going to kick all of the puppies. That's got to be it. It's evil—pure evil. And now P.E.T.A. is closing in on them!" Julianne knew that Chloe was mostly kidding, but she couldn't handle the Moore-bashing any longer. It was exhausting. Chloe studied her sister's face. "What's wrong? Jules, are you okay? You don't look—"

"I'm just not sure he's such a bad guy after all," Julianne blurted out. "I think it's all just kind of . . . messy."

"Oh, Jules." Chloe sighed like a deflating beach ball. "Of *course* he's a bad guy. Look what they're doing next door."

"That's the thing, though," Julianne continued. "We had this talk at work today, and he was showing definite, concrete signs of having a soul. I think he may just be going along with his family because they're his family. Plus, his family seems kind of rough. His dad showed up at the site last week, and you wouldn't believe the things he was saying to Remi! He was awful. I have no doubt that his dad is a destroyer of all that is good, but I just don't think Remi's the same way. He said these *things*, Chloe, about making something meaningful and bigger than him that just felt really . . . true."

"Yeah, but philosophical differences and parental pressures aside here, Jules, he's still going along. Whether he's heart-and-soul on board or not, his loyalty is still with his family. What's your deal, Jules? I mean, I know you guys, like, had a moment at the Malibu party, but that was ages ago! Besides, what prompted this heart-to-heart anyway? It sounds totally manipulative, if you ask me. If I were you, I'd watch your back. He absolutely, positively can't be trusted."

"Watch my back? What do you think he's going to do, impale me with a solar panel? Don't you think you're being a bit melodramatic?" As soon as the words were out of Julianne's mouth, she realized how silly she'd been acting, sneaking around, spying on Remi. Julianne just didn't know how to explain her mixed feelings to Chloe.

"I'm not being melodramatic. I'm just being cautious," Chloe explained, choosing her words very precisely. "Did Dad tell you that Remi's parents were over here the other day while you were out painting?"

"No!" Julianne's eyebrows shot up to her hairline and she felt a cold sweat break out along her collarbone. "What did they want?"

"This is what I'm trying to tell you!" Chloe exclaimed, as though she were talking to a confused child. "We really can't trust these people. They offered to buy our house and the land from Dad. They were really, really pushy about it. Calling it an 'offer' is pretty generous."

"No way!" Julianne gasped again, the intake of breath sharper this time. "They didn't threaten Dad or anything, did they?"

"Nope, but they did basically everything but," Chloe said in a conspiratorial whisper. "It was more of a strong-arm than an offer. I mean, obviously Dad didn't cave, but they were really all over him."

"Oh God." Julianne breathed out a long, slow whistle. She closed her eyes. "Still, I really don't think Remi's like that, though."

"I wouldn't let my guard down if I were you," Chloe insisted. "These are the people who raised him. Just keep that in the back of your mind, okay?"

"I just don't understand why everything has to be so us-versus-them all the time," Julianne pressed, standing up and pacing across the room toward Chloe's massive oak bookshelves. She trailed her fingers across the rows of alphabetized spines, comforting herself with their familiar texture.

"Because that's what it is, Jules. This is definitively an us-versus-them situation. They want to do something completely self-serving that will really hurt us. We want to stop them. That's sort of what 'us versus them' means. There's no way to be neutral here. You can't compromise—you can't be on both teams!" Chloe's face was darkening.

"Yeah, I guess you're right," Julianne agreed, flopping onto the mattress and sinking back into the cushy nest of pillows on Chloe's bed. "You're one hundred percent right." Julianne knew she should actually feel as confident in her sister's assessment of the situation as she was pretending to. Chloe had an annoying little habit of always being right about everything. Still, Julianne couldn't get over the nagging feeling that there was much more to Remi Moore than his family. She cocked her head toward her sister before getting up and walking out of the room. It didn't matter what she said about Remi; Chloe's mind was made up, and there would be no convincing her. Julianne walked into her own room and clicked the door shut behind her.

Chapter Thirteen

✦

Julianne excitedly pushed her small cart over the bright purple carpeting lining the aisles of Palisades Design. Other than the beach, there was no place she'd rather be on a beautiful day than stocking up on art supplies—especially with no supervision and a company credit card. That morning, Bill had called her aside and told her that the owners of the eco-house had asked for another new design concept. Apparently, they wanted a local artist to hand paint ivy in the courtyard. Julianne was still beaming that Bill had suggested her.

As Jules cruised through the aisles of Palisades Design, she was beside herself. What could be better than an entire store devoted to art supplies? She tossed a few different colors of green paint for the ivy walls into her cart, and was checking out a terra cotta stain when she noticed a familiar ponytail bouncing across the aisle in front of her.

"Lucy! Hey!" Julianne said, tossing the stain into her cart for further consideration and dashing down the aisle to greet her friend. Even though Lucy's back was turned as she made her way up the scrapbooking aisle, Julianne instantly recognized her by her red hair, freckled arms, compact frame, and regulation Mean Bean work T-shirt. Julianne hadn't seen her in ages. During the school year, they ran into each other all the time. Lucy worked at the Mean Bean, Julianne's favorite Palisades coffee shop, and occasionally contributed a comic strip to the *Cliffview*, the school arts magazine that Jules co-edited. Since Julianne's failed attempt to track Lucy down at the Malibu beach party where she'd met Remi, though, they hadn't seen each other once this summer.

"Oh my God, Jules! Long time no see!" Lucy squealed, running over to hug her friend. "Have you been in hibernation, or what? It's been forever! Ohmygod, how's Kat? Has she run with the bulls yet?" Lucy looked great. Her summer tan brought out the sparkle in her green eyes, and she had paired her black work T-shirt (which Julianne actually loved for its logo of two dueling coffee beans) with a pair of skinny gray jeans and slip-on Vans printed with hearts, stars, rainbows, and skulls. Lucy took a step back to appraise Julianne. "You look awesome, babe."

"Thanks! You too." Julianne laughed. "Kat's doing great. She's in Madrid, though, not Pamplona. And I'm pretty sure she'd stay inside if she did see a bull, but it sounds like she's having the time of her life. How's your summer going?"

"Oh, it's been great." Lucy grinned. "Some work, some surfing, some partying. It's a nice combo. It would be better, though"—she paused dramatically and affected a stern look—"if we ever *saw* you. You need to come out sometime. You haven't been by the Bean once, and I haven't seen you at Fishtail, either." Fishtail was one of Pacific Palisades' many outdoor cafés, but it was a favorite among Julianne's friends because of its boardwalk seating, live music, and notoriously lax carding policies. "Lady, we've missed you!"

"I know! I've missed you guys, too. The summer has just been really . . . intense so far," Julianne finished thoughtfully.

"Well, *good* intense or *bad* intense?" Lucy queried, leaning against a shelf full of glitter letters as she awaited Julianne's answer.

"I mean, *mainly* good," Julianne decided as she said it. "I have this awesome job—I'm doing building and design stuff for this cool new eco-friendly house being built near downtown," she explained. "I'm actually doing a huge mural for the courtyard, starting today," she explained, gesturing toward her cart of art supplies. "I get to hang outside, paint, *and*"—she paused for dramatic effect, the way Chloe did whenever she referred to Julianne's job—"I'm the only girl on an entire crew of guys!"

"Sweet!" Lucy giggled. "The Bean could use a serious infusion of testosterone. We're, like, seventy-five percent female this summer. It's crazy. I mean, everyone's great, but it isn't exactly a breeding ground for love." Lucy rolled her green eyes playfully. "Speaking of love . . . spill, Kahn. Tell me everything."

"Sorry to disappoint, Luce, but there really isn't much to tell." Julianne shrugged.

"Fibber!" Lucy practically shrieked. "We don't see you all summer and there's no guy involved? There's no way."

"Fine." Julianne laughed grudgingly. "There may kind of be someone. I mean, sort of. A little."

"That's more like it. Details, please," Lucy prodded.

"Okay, so I met this guy, and he seemed really great," Jules started.

"At work?" Lucy asked.

"Well, sort of. I mean, I didn't meet him at work, but it turns out he's at work." Julianne chewed her lower lip ever so slightly as she spoke.

"That sounds complicated." Lucy pulled a tube of

cherry ChapStick out of the pocket of her jeans and applied it liberally.

"Yeah, that's the whole thing. And there's stuff going on with his family, and with *my* family, and who knows if it can even work . . ." Julianne could feel her voice rising with each word.

"But you like him, right?" Lucy gave Julianne a knowing grin.

"Oh my God, Luce, he's amazing. He's beyond fantastic. He's into architecture, so he's kind of artistic. And he just totally gets what I love so much about *my* art. And he's funny and thoughtful and, oh man, so, so hot." Julianne felt the corners of her mouth creeping up into a smile as she reached into her bag for her Nalgene and took a drink.

"Well then, that's the important part." Lucy was full-on smiling now. "If you're meant for each other, all the pieces will come together somehow. That's all. That's just how it is. No worries." She squeezed Julianne's hand. Julianne smiled back at her, feeling relieved and thrilled that someone had finally given her the green light to like Remi. "Anyway, I should probably head out," Lucy said, looking at her old-school oversize Swatch watch. "It's free-smoothie-sample day at the Bean, and they need all the help they can get." She hugged Julianne goodbye, grabbed some scrapbooking pages off the wall hooks, and headed back down the aisle before turning and calling back, "Hey, you should bring this mystery guy out with us sometime. Or, you know, at least bring yourself. *Call me!*"

Julianne decided to stop at home before heading back to the site, just to pick up her camera and her favorite paintbrushes. She preferred working with brushes that she already liked the feel of, plus she wanted her camera to document her progress on the mural for her portfolio. Julianne burst through the door of her house like a husband in a '50s sitcom.

"Oh, honey, I'm hoooome!" She could hear Chloe and her father murmuring in another room, but neither of them called back to her. "Hey!" she called out again. "I'm home!" Again, there was no response. Julianne wandered into the dining room and found Chloe and her dad sitting at opposite ends of their oval dining table, both looking like they'd just been through a natural disaster. Chloe's cheeks were tearstained, and Dad's eyes looked pale and empty. They were both staring in the general direction of a pile of papers that had been tossed into the center of the table. Julianne hadn't seen either of them look this lost since the doctors had told them that Mom's cancer was malignant. Her throat started to close up at the memory. She walked around the table and placed a hand on Chloe's shoulder, careful not to muss the lace of her sister's puff-sleeve shirt. "Hey," she murmured. "What's going on?" Chloe just shook her head.

Finally, their father spoke. "Court papers, Jules." Julianne felt all the blood drain from her body and she slumped against the arm of Chloe's chair. "The Moores' lawyer served us with papers today. They're suing us over our property rights."

"They can't do that!" Julianne burst out. "I'm sure they can't. They haven't even been here two months. Mom bought this house thirty years ago. The mortgage is paid off. They can't do that. There's no way."

"Jules, I'm not sure we can do anything," Chloe whispered. Julianne felt her heart plummet from her chest. They couldn't possibly have to leave the house where their parents were married, and where Julianne and Chloe were born. The house where their mom had died.

"No. Absolutely not," Julianne said, rising to her feet. She couldn't believe what she was hearing. This couldn't be happening. "No, they can't do this. This is ridiculous!"

"Girls, I am so sorry," their father whispered. "I don't know if there's a case here or not, but, either way, we don't have the money to fight it. I am so sorry. I am so, so sorry." Dad buried his head in his hands. Slowly, Chloe pushed her chair back from the table and went over to wrap her arms around her father.

"Daddy, it'll be okay," she whispered. "It'll all be okay."

Julianne felt like someone had poured gasoline down

her throat and dropped in a match. Her entire body was twitching, burning. She couldn't take it anymore. She couldn't just stand there and watch her family hurting. She raced out of the house—not even bothering to shut the door behind her—and ran down to the beach. The wind off the ocean was cold and sharp, and the sand felt unstable under her feet. She ran all the way down the beach, her feet rolling under her with every step, until she reached the edge of the water. She thought, vaguely, that the Moores would probably try to have her arrested if they found her down here. Silently, she dared them to try it. *Just go ahead,* she thought. Julianne stood there until what was left of the day had slipped by and night had begun to roll down onto the beach. She stared out at the ocean, a mass of darkening ripples against the rising moonlight. The reflection of the moon was tossed off the waves, like someone had drizzled the water with liquid gold.

She sat down at the edge of the ocean as the night sky deepened, her feet tucked under her and her arms wrapped tightly around herself. Almost imperceptibly, she began to whisper. She couldn't even hear the words forming. She felt ridiculous, but Julianne needed her mother right now, and the beach had always been their special place.

"Mom, please. I don't know what to do. I can't let them take us away from you. I don't know what to do."

Fat tears started to slip down Julianne's face and she knew she was babbling, but she couldn't stop calling out to her mother. "Mom, I don't know how to make it better. I don't know how to keep us together without you here to show me. What do I do?" Julianne put her head in her hands and just sat there, listening to the tide pumping in and out like a heartbeat. She wasn't expecting to hear from her mother, but breathing in and out in time to the pulse of the tides, she knew she wasn't alone.

Chapter Fourteen

✦

Julianne snapped awake when the weight of a hand touched her shoulder. She looked up to find the tousled brown hair and concerned face of Remi Moore. Silently, Remi sat down next to Julianne. Keeping her gaze on the ocean, she told him flatly, "I don't want to see you right now."

"So don't look at me. But you shouldn't be alone. It's almost midnight. You've obviously been crying. You're a total wreck. Someone should be here with you." Concern poured out of every syllable Remi spoke. "I came looking for you as soon as I heard about the papers."

"I don't need you trying to take care of me right now." Julianne's tone remained completely flat. She was shocked to hear her own voice sound so dull. "You've done enough already," she finished.

"Julianne, I . . . I don't even know what to say." Remi's voice was tinged with regret.

All of a sudden, Julianne's voice came coursing back into her body. She turned to him. "I don't want to hear how bad you feel, how sorry you are. I don't want to hear any of it. I am just so tired of this. I'm done. I can't walk around with all of this negativity and worry all of the time—it's going to consume me. I can't care anymore. I just can't."

The sand looked blue-gray, spilling out under the night sky. Julianne stared absently out at the ocean.

"I hate this." Remi's voice sounded like it was choking in his throat. "I . . . I hate this."

"What?" Julianne finally turned her head toward him and stared at his profile.

"I hate this. I hate everything about this situation," Remi repeated. He was tracing tiny circles in the sand. "There is nothing about this that feels okay to me right now. I mean, I love my dad. I know how important these plans are to him. He's a great architect and I hope I can be as successful as he is some day. But I don't want it to happen like this. It's not right. I hate looking out the window of my bedroom and seeing the landscape being chipped away every day. I hate that I can *already* see that, and I haven't even lived here three months. I hate what it's doing to you and your family. I hate that every time I see my parents, I think about what they're doing to you. I know it's not enough, and I know it probably doesn't matter, but Julianne, I am so, so sorry."

They sat there for a while, staring alternately at the ocean and the sand. Julianne didn't know what to say, but somehow, hearing Remi apologize made everything feel a little bit better. She knew it wasn't his fault—he was just as powerless as she was. Nonetheless, hearing him say the words meant something. It felt like there was *possibility* buried in there somewhere, like she had been right when she defended him to Chloe. She turned and looked at him, silent tears streaming down her cheeks.

"Julianne, I . . ." This time Remi was the one to stop himself. Starting again, haltingly, he looked down at the sand. "I wanted to give you something that wouldn't change. That you could have forever and no one could take away." She looked up at him, not understanding. "That's why—" He cleared his throat and tried again. "That's why I talked to the owners about commissioning you for the mural. I wanted you to have something perfect, and I couldn't think of anything more perfect than your art." He reached out and brushed a tear off of Julianne's cheek with the side of his hand. Julianne's eyes widened and the slightest hint of a smile flashed across her face. He rested his hand on the nape of her neck, buried under her hair, and pulled her close to him for a kiss. It was slower and sadder than their other beach kisses had been, but Julianne still felt the same electricity crackling between them.

"Remi, I . . ." Julianne put her hand on his chest, pushing him back. "Thank you. That's the most thoughtful thing anyone has ever done for me. It's amazing. But . . ." Her voice faltered and threatened to break. "Remi, I can't. I can't be with you. Not with the house and with work. I can't do this to Chloe and my dad. I can't lie to them. I mean, I won't. Why does it have to be so complicated?"

Before Julianne could finish her sentence, Remi leaned over and kissed her again. For just a second, his warm lips on hers made the entire world dissolve into nothing more than the lapping of the ocean. And this time, Julianne didn't push him away.

"Julianne, you have no idea how special you are," Remi said, gazing at her adoringly as she settled into his arms. "You're smart; you're funny. You're more talented than you think you are. I've never met someone who just . . ."

"You get me." They finished the thought together.

"I know. You understand me like no one ever has before . . ." Julianne trailed off.

"It's like we're meant to be together," Remi offered, his shining eyes fixing her gaze. Julianne leaned in and kissed him again.

Lucy's advice in the art store came rushing back to Julianne. *If you're meant for each other, all the pieces will come together somehow.* And Julianne knew it was true. She was meant for Remi, and he was meant for her. Really, truly, and absolutely.

"Remi," Jules said with renewed determination. "Everything that's going on with the building and the beach—it sucks, but it's not about us. It may be our families, but it's not us." She looked over at him and knew he understood. She leaned her head against his strong shoulder, shut her eyes, and listened to the ocean's heartbeat mixing with his.

Chapter Fifteen

✦

Julianne popped her head around the corner, checking to see if the coast was clear. Turning her head so quickly that she was whipped in the face by her own curls, she decided she was good to go and shimmied up the ladder. Halfway up, she heard a low wolf whistle from below and looked down.

Beau and Randy, two of the guys she worked with, were standing at the base of the ladder, smirking.

"Now, where would you be going in such a hurry, Jules?" Randy teased as Beau sang, "Jules and Remi, sitting in a tree . . ." under his breath.

"Very mature, you guys." Julianne grinned. "So glad to have such evolved, professional role models to look up to around here."

Ever since Mitch had spotted Remi kissing Jules outside the trailer a few days earlier, the news that they were a couple had spread like wildfire. Now it seemed like their relationship suddenly included two dozen construction workers. The "little sister" dynamic Julianne shared with them was now extending to Remi, who couldn't walk by a member of the crew without a friendly punch to the shoulder or tousle of his hair. Julianne had never heard someone called "champ" or "pal" by so many people in such a short span of time.

"Eh, we do what we can." Randy winked at her playfully before lowering his voice conspiratorially, "Just so you know, Bill's not in until after lunch today. Just sayin'."

Beau shook his head at Randy and then turned to Jules. "We should get back to, um, building something. But you have a *great* morning, kiddo. If you happen to run into our favorite project manager, do give him our best." He tipped an imaginary hat at Julianne, then strode off with Randy, chuckling.

Julianne laughed as they walked away, then took one last look around and scooted back up the ladder. She pushed the flat wood panel that separated the crawl space from the rest of the house aside and pulled her body up through the trap-door slat, into the makeshift attic. The wood and plaster for the walls had been filled in over the past few weeks, and Jules was glad to use the space to its full advantage. After a moment of panic, where Julianne's legs seemed to want to stay downstairs, acting completely independent of the rest of her body, she half-tumbled into the space. Wiping away sawdust, she turned to Remi and smiled. "Good morning."

Remi was sitting in the crawl space on an old tarp with boxes of Pop-Tarts on either side of him. "Good morning." He yawned, before reaching for the red thermos of coffee just beyond his right hand.

"Ooh, Pop-Tarts!" Julianne laughed, looking over at the boxes. "I just love a man who can cook."

Remi half-blushed as he ripped open a silver foil pack of Frosted Strawberry. "You're just lucky it's not some sort of special occasion. I don't think you could handle my cinnamon toast."

Julianne imagined Remi in a chef's hat and a checkered apron and had to suppress a giggle. "I think you're right. I'm not sure I'm ready for that. I may need to work up to it."

Their laughter was interrupted by the sound of work boots clomping underneath them. They both froze, holding their breath out of habit. The footsteps lingered, and Julianne was afraid she would pass out from holding her breath so long, but she was more afraid of making any noise by breathing out. Next to her, Remi had frozen in mid-reach, twisted up like some sort of human pretzel.

"Don't fall!" Julianne whispered under her breath as the footsteps started to fade away.

Remi, already shaking a little from the effort of squeezing himself into hiding mode, did exactly that. He stayed sprawled out on his back, silently shaking with laughter for the next couple minutes. Julianne crawled over and placed herself gingerly next to him, careful not to make any noise that could draw unwanted attention to the attic, just in case the guys were wrong about Bill. She knew that the crew had their backs, but she also didn't want to test that theory. She rolled over in almost mimelike slow motion to look at Remi. "Next time," she breathed, "I think we should just go out for bagels."

✦ ✦ ✦

For the second time in one summer, work was turning into *Ocean's 14*. Jules and Remi spent all day waiting for stolen moments to see each other. Julianne used her well-honed spy skills to scout out any opportunity to catch Remi alone—even for five minutes. Remi requested lots of "consultations" with Julianne to discuss her progress on painting the ivy in the courtyard. Every time Julianne walked into the trailer, the guys hooted and hollered. Most of the time, though, despite the support of the crew, they avoided even looking at each other. Julianne and Remi were both afraid that if they made eye contact, they wouldn't be able to stop staring, and they'd never get any work done ever again. In the trailer, they tried to keep things as professional as possible, but even the accidental touch of their hands caused them to forget all the official business they were supposed to be plotting out.

Between their warring families, and the constant procession of lawyers, co-workers, and even Bill, it seemed like every bit of their time was spent trying to deal with what other people's reactions to their relationship might be. Neither Jules nor Remi was sure what, exactly, would happen if their respective families found out that they were together, but they were both sure that it would turn their summer romance into a Shakespearean tragedy.

Chapter Sixteen

✦

Julianne tiptoed toward the front door. Even though it was early evening and still light out, she felt like she was making an escape under cover of darkness. She already had one hand outstretched toward the waiting doorknob when she heard a quiet sound—almost a purring—over her right shoulder. She wheeled around to find Chloe there, clearing her throat softly.

"And where are *you* going, young lady?" Chloe's voice was light, teasing, but Julianne could tell the question wasn't entirely a joke.

"Oh, just down to the beach. Meeting up with Lucy and some of the guys from the site. We might wind up at Lucy's later, or maybe the Fishtail . . ." Julianne trailed off, trying to make the details of her plans sound especially mundane. She didn't want to lie to Chloe any more than was totally necessary.

"Some guys from the site, or a particularly *special* guy from the site?" Chloe teased, clicking her tongue against her teeth.

Julianne's heart raced. "Like who?" she asked, trying to be nonchalant.

"Like who? Like anyone! You work with two dozen hot guys, it's almost impossible to narrow the field." Chloe giggled.

"Sorry, Chloe. Not a date. Just hanging out." Julianne felt bad for the half-truths, but, really, it *wasn't* a date. She couldn't wait until she and Remi were actually able to go on dates like other couples. But all this sneaking around was decidedly *not* dinner and a movie.

"Darn. Okay, well have fun." Chloe shrugged before adding, "I was over at the Fishtail the other night and the band was really good." She headed for the steps, and Julianne completed her beeline for the door.

Julianne walked down the beach, flip-flops in hand, her stomach doing a few funny little jumps every now and then. She couldn't tell if she was just having excitement butterflies because she was going to see Remi—just the thought of spending time with him was enough to make her totally giddy—or if they were little pangs of guilt from lying to Chloe. After a few minutes, though, they went away entirely and so did the question. After walking for what felt like forever, she saw the familiar shape of Remi's tousled hair and broad shoulders. Julianne broke into a sprint and dashed toward him. Plopping herself down on the sand, she laughed and mock-gasped for breath.

"I feel like I've been walking for six hours. How did you find this place? I've lived here all my life and barely knew it existed." She linked one arm through Remi's and leaned in close. When they had decided they should try to meet farther away from their respective houses, Remi had, in true project manager style, undertaken a massive site search. As a result, they were now sitting on an out-of-the-way stretch of beach silhouetted by craggy sloping cliffs. The sunset coming down around the cliffs and breaking through the bowing palm trees was amazing. Julianne sighed happily. It was totally worth the nearly forty-five minutes she had walked to get here.

Remi squeezed her hand. "I know. It's pretty random, isn't it? But it's so beautiful. The cliffs are amazing."

"The cliffs aren't the only thing that's amazing," Julianne said softly, squeezing his hand in return.

"Yeah, you are pretty great, aren't you?" Remi responded seriously, but there was a laugh in his voice.

"I wasn't talking about *me*, and you know it!" Julianne laughed back, before being pulled into a giant bear hug. Between the towering cliffs and Remi's strong arms, she had rarely felt so safe and so warm.

Julianne was pretty sure that this stolen time was worth all the sneaking around. More than once, Remi had driven over to Palisades Design and waited in the back by the oil paints so he and Julianne could see each other while she picked up supplies to finish her mother's painting. Those few minutes alone, not hiding from anyone or anything, completely justified all the times they felt like sketchy stalkers hiding in the bushes outside of a celebrity's house.

At work, both Julianne and Remi tried to keep a low profile. Partially because the teasing could get embarrassing, but mainly because they didn't want the guys to have to lie to Bill—no matter how many times the crew offered to keep an eye out on their behalf. Julianne spent a lot of time in the courtyard working on the mural, or laying down tiles or solar panels. Remi tried to keep himself constantly busy elsewhere, doing daily check-ins with Bill and seeing if any of the guys had overflow projects they needed help with. Remi also had a special project of his own that he was planning for the house, and he spent his lunch breaks holed up in the trailer with a pencil and graph paper, planning it out. Julianne did have to admit, though, now that she was scared of getting caught, she was a million times more productive at work. She had never been more focused in her life.

But now they sat staring at the ocean. The sunset had

melted into evening, but the water was still shining just as beautifully as ever. Every so often, the quiet on the beach was punctuated by a burst of laughter or a happy sigh and Julianne felt like she could stay here forever. Then her moment of bliss was interrupted by the sharp beep of her cell phone ringing. She dug into the pocket of her shorts, pulled out the phone, and looked at the display. It was Lucy.

"Hello?"

"Jules? Where are you? You were supposed to meet us an hour ago!" Lucy didn't sound annoyed, just a little worried.

"Oh, damn! Luce, I totally lost track of time. I am so sorry!" Julianne jumped up from the ground and brushed a dusting of sand off of her legs.

"Don't worry about it. I figured you were probably painting and spaced out for a while. You're still coming out, though, right?" Lucy asked.

"Totally. Of course! I'll be there as soon as I can. Tell the guys I'm sorry!" Julianne felt awful. She had been so excited about sneaking off with Remi before meeting her friends that she had forgotten about the actual *meeting her friends* part.

"No worries, Jules. We'll see you soon," Lucy chirped.

Julianne clicked her phone shut and looked over at Remi, who was shaking his head knowingly. "I knew we forgot something." He laughed. "I'm supposed to meet some of the guys from the site in fifteen minutes for night soccer."

Julianne shook her head as she shook off her flip-flops. "Remington Moore, why do you have to be so distracting?" she teased.

Remi chuckled. "I could say the same for you, lady. Hey, do you need a ride to meet your friends? I'm parked over at a shopping center down the road."

"That would be great. Only . . ." Julianne blushed.

"Only what?" Remi asked, his eyes crinkling.

"Only, could you maybe drop me off a few blocks away and I'll walk the rest of the way myself?" Julianne looked down, a little embarrassed that Remi had made such a sweet offer and she wasn't able to entirely take him up on it.

"No problem. I used to make my parents do that when they would drop me off at school when I was a kid." Remi laughed his warm laugh, and Julianne's whole body relaxed. She could listen to him laugh forever. He slipped his hand around hers and led her to the car.

Hours later, Julianne was walking down the beach near her house on the way back from hanging out with Lucy, Mitch, and Hunter. The night had been a blast—Frisbee on the beach, checking out a band at the Fishtail—and her late entrance hadn't put the smallest crimp in the fun. Despite her awesome mood, she couldn't help but stop and stare as she passed Remi's house. She knew he wasn't home—his soccer game hadn't started until after she met up with her friends, and those guys could play all night—but it didn't look like anyone else was home either. Julianne thought it was odd. For a massive glass compound, there were very rarely people visible in the windows. She wondered if anyone was ever home over there, other than Remi, or if Mr. and Mrs. Moore were holed up someplace else while the house was being *enlarged*. The thought made Julianne instantly annoyed. As much as she didn't blame Remi, she still couldn't forgive his parents for what they were doing with their gigantic McMansion. And to think that they were going through all of this trouble—with the lawyers and the papers and the near daily pressure of offers and threats levied at the Kahns to sell their land—and they weren't even living there? It was a worse thought than she could stand. Shrugging the tension out of her shoulders and allowing the good mood her night out had put her into return, Julianne turned her eyes away from the Moores' house and walked the rest of the way home in the warm summer air.

She slipped quietly through the back door, making as little noise as possible. She wasn't being sneaky this time; she just didn't want to wake anyone. As she crept to the landing on her way up to her room, she noticed that a ribbon of light was escaping from under Chloe's door. She climbed the stairs and paused for a moment outside of her sister's room. If Chloe were asleep after all, she would pop her head in and turn out the light for her. As Julianne stood there, she could hear Chloe's teary, panicked voice on the phone. Julianne shook her head sadly—she knew *exactly* what Chloe was crying to her friends about—but she turned away and headed into her bedroom anyway. There was nothing she could do to help her sister tonight, and she needed to rest for work in the morning.

As far as Julianne was concerned, work was both the best and the worst part of this summer. On one hand, anything that kept her away from the tension at home was a good thing. Between the constant harassment from the Moores' lawyers, her dad walking around the house like a zombie, and Chloe's constant careening among normal Chloe, desperate crying Chloe, and Chloe-who-was-determined-to-fix-everything-and-comfort-everybody, Julianne felt like she was living in some bizarre, alternative universe. The only thing that felt constant was Remi, but with his comfort came the need to act like neither knew the other one existed ninety-eight percent of the time. On the other hand, a huge portion of the time that Remi and Jules needed to avoid each other was at work. So every weekday they had the opportunity to see each other was also a day in which they had to pretend they couldn't care less that the other one was around—or risk getting busted by Bill or ribbed by the guys from the crew at an inopportune moment.

✦ ✦ ✦

The following morning she was out in the courtyard sitting up on top of a ladder, working on her ivy mural. She felt like some sort of queen holding court—every few minutes, someone would pop their head into the courtyard, stand at the bottom of the ladder, and compliment her on how well everything was coming together, how professional it looked, or how much the owners were going to love it. Perched on top of her ladder in her paint-stained cutoffs, a black-paint-splattered T-shirt, and her new pink retro Pumas, with her oversize sunglasses obscuring half her face, Julianne felt (at least for that moment) like she was doing everything she could have hoped to do with her summer. With every brushstroke, she counted one thing that was going even *better* than she could have hoped. Stroke—she had an awesome job. Stroke—where she got to spend all day outside. Stroke—working with her hands. Stroke—on something really cool. Stroke—and, sometimes, even painting. Stroke—for money. Stroke—only a few feet away from one of the most amazing guys she'd ever met.

As if on cue, Remi popped his head out into the

courtyard. His sneak attacks had lost their effect now that he and Julianne knew each other well enough to anticipate the other's next move.

"Hey!" he called up the ladder. "How's the painting going?"

"Why don't you come up here and tell me?" Julianne called back down. Remi shimmied up the ladder two rungs at a time, until his face was almost level with Julianne's. "So, what do you think?" she asked, tilting her head down toward him.

"Brilliant," Remi assured her, his dark eyes darting from wall to wall, surveying Julianne's work. Julianne could tell from the way his eyes brightened as he looked around the courtyard that he liked what he saw. "Wherever can I find the gentleman who discovered such sparkling local talent? Clearly he's a genius with discriminating taste." He looked up at Jules and grinned. She had never met anyone who grinned like that. It made her feel dizzy and warm.

Julianne arched her eyebrows and shrugged. "I don't know. It's going to be pretty hard to track him down. I heard he used to be a project manager around here, but they had to let him go because he was always slacking off and hanging around with his girlfriend."

"Poor guy," Remi said quietly, looking down the ladder.

"I know," Julianne answered wryly. "But, for what it's

worth, I heard that the girlfriend was totally hot, if that makes you feel any better."

"You know, oddly enough, it does. Actually, I heard that, too." Remi ran his fingers over Julianne's cheekbone. "She was gorgeous. And insanely talented."

Julianne laughed and rolled her eyes. "I'm sure this guy must have had *something* going for him, to get together with her."

"Not much. Mainly, he was charming." Remi laughed. Then he reached up, rested his hand on the back of Julianne's head, and kissed her. As soon as their lips touched, Julianne heard a noise in the doorway. Remi quickly hopped up another rung on the ladder and leaned over Jules's shoulder, pretending to admire the detail work on a section of the painting.

Julianne peered down around Remi to see who'd come into the courtyard. Bill Cullen was standing at the bottom of the ladder, looking bemused. "What are you guys up to?" he asked.

"Bill, have you seen the detail work on Julianne's painting here?" Remi asked thoughtfully. "It's . . . very impressive. The client is going to be really thrilled." He climbed down a few rungs of the ladder before turning his eyes back to Julianne. "Keep up the great work," he said as neutrally as possible. He hopped off the ladder and turned back to Bill again. "It's really . . . just great."

Bill raised one graying eyebrow. "Jules is great. That's

not news to me," he said matter-of-factly. Then he turned and headed out of the courtyard, calling over his shoulder, "Lunch break's at one-thirty today. If you want pizza, it's three bucks."

It wasn't until Bill had left that Julianne felt the heat leave her face and noticed the green paint smeared on Remi's shirt. They exchanged a quick, panicked look and Remi mouthed, "Do you think he knows?"

Julianne shrugged and whispered, "Maybe?"

The near miss was enough to put them both on edge. Remi shifted his weight from one foot to the other while Julianne twisted the same piece of hair around her finger over and over again.

"Um, well, okay. 'Bye," Remi blurted, dashing out of the courtyard.

"Yeah, 'bye," Julianne replied, but even as he hurried away, she couldn't take her eyes off him.

Chapter Seventeen

✦

Julianne couldn't believe she was finally putting the finishing touches on her mom's painting. And just in time. After a week of beautiful weather, a patch of clouds was rolling in over the Palisades, bringing an unusual gray with it. Julianne dabbed a few final highlights of gold on the canvas, just to make the beach come that much more alive. Ever since that night she spent out on the beach listening for her mom a few weeks earlier, it was like all the pieces of her painting had suddenly started falling into place. The light was just right, and her colors had become richer, deeper, and more complex, somehow. It was like Hannah Kahn was out there somewhere, telling Jules to take her gifts and run with them, and if Jules just listened closely enough, she'd know what she was supposed to do. Grinning at her finished painting, Julianne practically hugged herself with delight over her accomplishment. She grabbed the painting off its easel and rushed it inside and up to her bedroom, where it could dry without the threat of sudden raindrops.

When Julianne woke up the next morning, the gray skies were still in full effect, and the gloom wouldn't dissipate. That whole weekend—the weekend of the anniversary of Hannah Kahn's death—it was unusually dark and drizzly for summertime in LA. Julianne, Chloe, and Dad sat around the living room in equally gray moods. They had watched old family videos and played three consecutive games of Trivial Pursuit (at which Chloe had thoroughly schooled Julianne and her father, three consecutive times), but the prevailing mood in the Kahn household was still listing toward melancholy.

"Who starred in the eponymous show about a newscaster in Minneapolis?" Chloe asked, yawning.

"Oh, even I know this one," muttered Dad. "Mary Tyler Moore."

"Chloe, do we really have to go through the additional cards?" Julianne whined. "We already played the game."

"Do you have any better recreational suggestions?" Chloe countered, probably not meaning to sound quite so snippy. "Shall we do dramatic readings from the latest

Publishers Weekly?" Chloe drawled, holding up a copy of their dad's magazine. "Or should we watch another movie that we've all seen five times? Now that would be fun."

Julianne looked at her sister and yawned. She curled her feet under her on the oversize couch and flopped back, peeling a split end in her hair. "I could always make popcorn. Or we could play Pictionary."

"No Pictionary," her father pleaded. "I've already been humiliated on the board game battlefield by one daughter today. I'm not going back for seconds."

Unable to reach consensus, they drifted to separate parts of the house. Dad went into his studio and Chloe clomped upstairs, while Julianne stayed put in the living room.

Julianne kept watch out the window for a break in the unseasonably dreary weather. She had wrapped her painting in butcher paper and hidden it under her bed. She'd been hoping to give it to Dad and Chloe today, but her grand plan required sunshine. So she remained at her post in the window seat, looking out over the beach with a book in her lap.

At the first hint of sun, Jules jumped at her chance.

"*Daaaad! Chloe!* Come in here!" She knew her dad was getting things together for a meeting with his editor in New York next week, and Chloe was talking on the phone with one of her sorority sisters, but time was of the essence.

Julianne dashed upstairs, skipping every other step, and bounded into Chloe's room, not caring in the slightest if she was interrupting an important phone call. "Chloe Elise Kahn, you have five minutes to get your butt downstairs and out onto the back deck!"

Chloe put her hand over the receiver and looked at Julianne, her hazel eyes questioning and mildly annoyed. "What's wrong?" she mouthed.

"Nothing's wrong, but it's important." Julianne wheedled.

"Now?" Chloe mouthed. *"Really?"*

"Really! Now go. Go, go, go! And get Dad on your way out." Julianne pivoted on her heel and burst toward the hallway.

Before Chloe had a chance to argue, Julianne ran into her room and closed the door behind her. She got down on her hands and knees and wedged herself under her bed, reaching for the wrapped canvas. She finally got her hands around it and gently wiggled it out. Then she walked over to her white wicker bookshelves. Sharing space with dozens of art books and a complete collection of her dad's children's books were a half-dozen framed family photos. Julianne took her favorite down from the shelf. It was beginning to yellow and fold up around the edges with age. It was a shot of Julianne and her mother on the beach by their house, when Julianne was two or three. They had matching mother/daughter easels. Hannah had started a beautiful beachscape on hers, and Julianne's easel was smeared with finger-paint—not to mention the paint all over her face, streaked on her bathing suit, and splashed on her little toddler bonnet. Her mother looked stunning—she was wearing a floppy hat and oversize sunglasses, with a paintbrush clenched between her teeth—and she was chasing after little Jules, who was about to make a mad dash for the water.

Julianne spent a minute with the photo, looking at herself, looking at her mom, before placing it gently back on the shelf. She picked up her canvas and headed downstairs.

When Julianne stepped outside, the sun was still shining and her father and sister were looking at her like she'd gone completely bonkers.

"Sweetie, are you all right?" her father said, breaking the ice.

Julianne looked back and forth between her father and Chloe. "I'm sorry for being such a drama queen, but I have something for you guys, and it is really important that I show it to you while the sun is still shining, or it just wouldn't be right."

She handed the wrapped canvas to her father, who took a seat next to Chloe on the deck. As Dad and Chloe unwrapped the brown paper together, Julianne watched the corners of her father's mouth curl up in a sad smile. Chloe was grinning from ear to ear.

"Oh my God! It's amazing. It's beyond amazing," she gushed.

"Mom started this before she got sick and I wanted you guys to have it." Julianne gestured to the beach beyond the deck. "Now we'll always have Mom and we'll always have our beach."

"Julianne, it's so different from your other collaborations with your mother," her father observed, sounding pleased that his little girl had grown up to have such artistic range.

Jules nodded. "I guess so. It was really hard for me, actually. But I think it turned out okay."

"It turned out better than okay," Chloe gushed. "And like you said, we'll always have the beach, just as Mom saw it." Even though an undertone of sadness gripped all three of them, the Kahns shared a warm smile.

Julianne walked over to her father and threw her arms around his shoulders and said, "I'm glad you like it, Dad."

As the beginnings of tears collected in the corners of Edward Kahn's eyes, he hugged his daughter back and whispered, "Thank you."

Chapter Eighteen

✦

The music at the Fishtail was pumping at earsplitting volume and Julianne felt her body shaking in time with the bass. She and Remi had been out for hours. It felt so good to just hang out and be a couple without stressing over who might be watching. Even if they technically were the *only* ones who knew they were out as a couple. After work, they'd headed to happy hour with some of the guys from the crew, at a bar farther down the boardwalk. After happy hour, Mitch and Hunter in tow, they'd stopped by the Mean Bean to pick up Lucy and head over to the Fishtail to meet more friends from school. So many weeks of relative isolation had left Julianne beyond excited to be out on the town with her friends *and* her amazing new (secret) boyfriend. She wished Kat were there—she was sure that Kat and Remi would totally hit it off—but then they'd have some time to hang out together when Kat got back from Madrid in a few weeks.

Julianne surveyed the scene at the Fishtail. It was her favorite kind of boardwalk party, high energy and low key at the same time. Hunter, Mitch, and Remi were standing against the boardwalk railing, talking about colleges, while Lucy and Jules were perched on top of a picnic table, watching the scene unfold. Down on the beach there were a few clusters of night swimmers and kids playing volleyball, but most of the action was contained on the boardwalk. The waves were rolling into shore and they could hear the breeze blowing the palm trees. Seagulls were winging their way across the horizon.

"I love summer." Jules sighed, taking a sip of the piña colada she was sharing with Lucy.

"I know, right?" Lucy agreed. "I just wish it would last longer. I can't even start thinking about school—I have too much to do before then."

As they spoke, Justin Timberlake's voice came thumping out of the speakers. Jules grabbed her friend's hand and pulled Lucy down from the table. "Don't think, then!" she shouted over the music. "Just dance!"

The girls laughed as they jumped up and down, winding their bodies to the beat. "Way to bring sexy back!"

Julianne laughed at Lucy, who was dropping it all the way down to the floor.

"Um, I don't think sexy ever left . . ." Lucy joked back, jabbing Julianne with her elbow. "Speaking of which, I'm going to go introduce myself to those guys over there." She headed off to chat with a group of cute guys Jules vaguely recognized from school, who were shooting pool by the outdoor bar. Looking around the party, Julianne couldn't help but notice that several other girls were admiring her boyfriend, and she laughed to herself. Then she looked down at her outfit—a Proenza Schouler tank top with a deep V-neck and funky buttons, a swingy skirt, and turquoise open-toed Seychelles slip-ons—and felt pretty hot herself. Her hair was curly, wild, and blowing in the ocean breeze. Julianne tossed her head back and tried to soak everything in, waiting a long minute before heading down the boardwalk to catch up with Lucy. She glanced behind and caught Remi full-on staring at her. Maybe forced separation could be a little fun.

After a few hours, the party began to wind down, with couples strolling off in pairs and kids riding off on their bikes in every direction. Julianne and Lucy were dancing with some of Lucy's co-workers from the Mean Bean and a few of the younger guys from the site, when Remi walked over and slid his arm around Jules's waist.

"Ready to head out?" he whispered into her curls. She nodded and looked to her friends, who all looked ready to call it a night. Together, still bobbing their heads to the music, they all headed home.

Mitch and Hunter drifted away from the group first, to go meet up with some of the other guys from the cross-country team for a poker game; then Lucy's co-workers left one by one. As Lucy, Julianne, and Remi made their way down the beach toward Lucy's grandparents' house, Lucy leaned over and tipsily stage-whispered in Julianne's ear, "So, is this *the boyfriend*?"

"Huh?" Julianne was confused.

"The guy you were telling me about at the art store," Lucy clarified louder. "The hottie you've had your eye on all summer?"

Julianne blushed, even in the darkness. Even perfectly sober, subtlety had never been Lucy's strong point. "Yup. He's the one."

"You're right, Jules. He's cute—really cute!" Lucy giggled. "Oh my gosh, I almost missed my house." Lucy looked up sheepishly before dashing off for home. "Good night, you guys! Nice to meet you, Remi," she practically cooed.

Remi finally slipped his hand into Julianne's, and they walked the rest of the way down the beach together, stopping to sit down in the sand when they reached the stretch of beach between their two houses. Half an hour later, Julianne and Remi were lying on their backs, looking up at the stars. The weather had stayed clear all night, despite a threat of rain, and the sky was absolutely the most intense shade of navy blue that Julianne had ever seen. Normally, she would have been trying to figure out exactly how to mix the color of the sky, how to capture it. Tonight, however, she was too distracted by Remi's hand resting on her stomach. Her entire body felt like it had been hit by lightning. As soon as Remi touched her skin, there wasn't a single part of her that wasn't hypercharged and tingling. It was almost as though she needed to either stay perfectly still or risk her entire body bursting into flames.

Remi rolled over and propped his head up on Julianne's stomach. "What are you thinking, Jules?" He kissed her belly button, and Julianne felt her skin ignite again.

Julianne ran her fingers through Remi's brown hair, which was getting scruffier by the day. "I'm thinking about the sky. Can you figure out what color that is?"

Remi stared up and tried in earnest for a few minutes to figure it out. "Nope. Can't say I can. But I also don't think that's what you were thinking about. Try again?"

Julianne laughed softly and continued playing with his hair. It wasn't as soft as it looked, but it was surprisingly fluffy. Downy, almost. She thought she would be perfectly content just weaving her fingers in and out of it all night. She looked down and saw that Remi's big eyes were staring up at her, filled with a mix of curiosity and expectation. "Are you actually still asking me?"

Remi nodded.

"You're really going to make me say it?"

Remi nodded again.

"Okay, fine." Julianne rolled her eyes. "I was thinking about your hair, okay?"

Even Remi looked a little surprised at this one. "What?" Julianne challenged. "You have very nice hair; it's a very interesting texture."

Remi rolled back over and buried his face against Julianne's stomach. "I love dating an artist," he mumbled, laughing. Julianne sat up, like she'd been hit with a sudden inspiration. Jolted by the movement, Remi shot up after her. "Hey!" Julianne squealed. "I have a good idea."

"What?" he asked gamely.

"How about you come here and kiss me?" She grinned.

"You don't need to ask me twice." Remi pulled himself up from the ground with a laugh.

Soon they were rolling over each other in the sand, laughing and kissing the kind of slow, greedy kisses that go on for days. They kissed like they were trying to breathe each other's air. Julianne felt Remi's tongue in her mouth, soft but insistent, like he was determined to find out more, but willing to take all the time in the world to do it. She ran her hands up and down his spine, tracing the muscles of his back. Jules remembered her surprise at seeing him in his towel in the trailer and blushed. Julianne hadn't been surprised at all by what a great kisser he was—not even the first time they'd kissed at the party—but she was pleasantly surprised that every single time they kissed, it got better and better. Julianne's tank top had slid up around her rib cage, and Remi bent to kiss her stomach and run his fingers along her sternum. She buried her face in his neck, and was kissing the side of his jawbone. Then she heard something moving farther up the beach.

She nudged Remi and hissed urgently, "Someone's coming." Remi's already-huge eyes grew as big as Frisbees as he catapulted himself at least five feet away from her. "Nice air!" she whispered, grinning up to his standing figure.

Remi pointed to his sweater, which was sitting to Jules's left. A minute ago, it had been tucked under her head while they looked at the sky. "Toss it somewhere!" Remi whispered, before subtly blowing her a kiss and taking off down the beach as though he were out for a night run. Julianne smoothed down her shirt and hair and tucked her legs under her, staring out at the ocean. Absentmindedly, she began making piles of sand around her legs, transferring little bits from one pile to the other and back again.

The footsteps got closer, and Julianne was aching to turn around and see who had busted up her make-out session with Remi, but she was afraid of blowing her cover.

Chapter Nineteen

✦

When the footsteps were directly behind her, Julianne tossed a casual glance over her shoulder just in time to see Chloe slide down next to her. Chloe's coffee-colored hair was pulled into a high, tight ponytail, and she was wearing her teal Kappa Delta T-shirt and a pair of light blue seagull-printed pajama pants.

Chloe's eyes scanned the beach and Julianne thought she saw her sister squint at the sight of the figure that was now a few hundred yards down the beach, moving at a steady jog. But if Chloe saw anyone, she didn't say anything. She just pulled her legs up to her chest and turned her head toward Julianne.

"Cute outfit," Chloe said.

"Thanks." Julianne smiled at her sister.

"Nice to know that even without my styling you, you can come up with something nice." Chloe giggled. "So, was the Fishtail hopping?"

"Oh, Chloe, it was ridiculous, totally packed." Jules leaned in to fill her sister in on that night's party. "There was an awesome DJ and a ton of cute guys—even some we didn't already know." She laughed at the closeness of their town. "I think Lucy got, like, three new phone numbers."

Chloe laughed. "And you? Did you add anything to your little black book?"

"Not so much. I wasn't really there looking, if you know what I mean," Julianne answered.

"I have absolutely no idea what you mean. These days, I'm always looking!"

"Well, the Fishtail was an awesome place to look tonight," Julianne conceded. "Everyone was dancing. There was so much energy. Some freshman girls followed Mitch and Hunter around all night, just giggling at them. It was hilarious. Every time we turned around, there they were. But they never said a word!"

"Oh man." Chloe laughed. "Do you remember when that was us? Watching senior guys pass by in the hallway at school and just totally losing it?"

"I know! Mitch even went up and asked them their names, and they just giggled and ran away." Julianne leaned in closer to her sister, still laughing. "I thought Lucy was going to make them name tags or something."

"It sounds like it was fun." Chloe sighed. "Much better than filling out charts all night."

"You'll have to come with us next time. It'll be great!" Julianne promised.

Julianne linked her arm through her sister's. She couldn't have been happier to be sitting on the beach with her best friend in the world after a fabulous night, with one glaring exception. She felt gross not telling Chloe about Remi. Right now, they were the two most important people on Earth to her, and she would have loved it if they could somehow get along. She had a feeling they would, if Chloe could forget he was a Moore. Save for some pilfered Halloween candy when she was eight, Julianne had never hidden anything from her sister before. It made her feel dirty.

Chloe's voice jolted Julianne out of her reverie. "Let's talk more about your night!"

"Okay," Julianne replied enthusiastically. "What haven't we covered? So, the Fishtail was packed, the music was great, people were dancing. It was really fun."

"The guys were cute?" Chloe reaffirmed.

"Definitely," Julianne answered, though her thoughts centered around one cute guy in particular.

"I haven't been out in *for*-ever," Chloe enunciated. "All I do these days is work. I don't think I've been to a party since Malibu."

"Yeah . . ." Julianne trailed off noncommittally. She

was realizing that her promise to go out with her sister next time around might not work if she wanted to see Remi, too.

"Can I ask you a question?" Chloe asked thoughtfully. Julianne felt her heart sink. She couldn't have a heart-to-heart with Chloe right now. Not when there was something so big that she couldn't share.

"Yup?" Julianne squeaked.

"How would you feel about having a little soiree next week?" Chloe suggested conspiratorially.

"While Dad is in New York?" Jules was hesitant—she already had way too many secrets in her life right now.

"You, my dear, are a mind reader. You know, like a bringing-down-the-house party?" Chloe pressed on, full steam ahead.

"A what?" Julianne had no idea what Chloe meant.

"A bringing-down-the-house party. You know, if the Moores are going to level our house anyway, then we ought to throw it quite the goodbye shindig." Julianne felt her heart thud to her feet. Her pulse was racing.

"But wouldn't Dad be pretty pissed off if we get to keep the house after all and there's nothing left but a post-party pile of stones and beams?" Julianne focused on the mounds of sand she was still transferring from leg to leg.

"Fair enough," Chloe answered thoughtfully. "I was halfway joking, anyway."

Julianne rested her head against her sister's shoulder.

Her heart was still racing with the stress of being dishonest. "I know," she said softly.

"So, tell me more about the Fishtail," Chloe chirped. "Who was there, who was single?"

"Um, Hunter and Mitch," Julianne began.

"Yeah, but you run with them. They don't count. They're too sibling-y to make out with. Who else?" Chloe pressed on.

"Oh, I don't know. Some surfers. Some guys playing pool—Lucy was really into them." Julianne wished this conversation would just stop, somehow.

"Hmm. Definite potential," Chloe declared. "Anyone really catch your eye, though? Anyone special?"

This was becoming torturous. "No one new." Julianne answered, choosing her words deliberately so that she wasn't lying, exactly. She thought she and Chloe had covered all of this already.

"Well, just meeting new guys is half the battle," Chloe said supportively. "I know it was tough for you to get over McMansion Jr., but I'm really glad you did. It's good to see you going out and meeting new guys."

Julianne was silent.

"Jules, you know I'm proud of you, right?" Chloe's words were like salt in a huge cut on her sister's heart.

"That painting was really amazing, you know," Chloe said after a moment of silence.

Julianne smiled at her sister. "Thanks."

"Have you given any thought to applying to schools yet?" Jules could tell that her sister, always the organizer and the achiever, was gearing up for a big Jules-goes-to-college push.

"Sure," Julianne said. "I mean, you know, some. Nothing really serious. I've been sort of . . . occupied with other things this summer."

"No, totally. I understand that." Chloe nodded. "But you should really check out some art schools. You're incredible—you'll be beating off recruiters with a stick."

"Oh yeah. That's the best way to get a full ride to college, ya know," Julianne teased. "I'll definitely bring a stick along to all my campus interviews."

Chloe giggled. "I think that's what they mean by taking the college application process into your own hands. Beat them into submission and so on."

"You never miss a beat, do you Chloe?" Julianne laughed at her own bad joke.

"Oh God, we really are related." Chloe snorted. "Please tell me we don't pun alike. I think we Kahn girls may be genetically not funny."

"I'm afraid it's true," Jules agreed—but she couldn't help but laugh.

Chapter Twenty

✦

"Aw yeah!" Randy called as Julianne and Remi walked toward the staircase to the basement, tiles crammed into their tool belts, cement and spreaders in either hand. "If the bathroom's a rockin', don't come a'knockin'."

"Oh, *stop!*" Julianne laughed. "Remi and I are just going to lay some tile."

"Well that's a shame, darlin'," Randy replied. As Julianne followed Remi downstairs, she heard Randy chuckling to himself.

Crammed into the tiny auxiliary bathroom in the basement of the eco-house, safely hidden from the torrential rains outside, Remi reached for a tile across Julianne's lap and (maybe not so accidentally) brushed across her thigh.

Every time he got anywhere near her, Julianne felt like she'd just walked into a really pleasant bug zapper. Everything flashed blue and electric and she had to double check to make sure that she was still breathing. She pulled herself together long enough to raise a sly eyebrow and tease, "Excuse me, Mr. Moore. A responsible project manager keeps his hands to himself." She laughed at her own mock-saucy voice.

Remi shot back a sexy, "Oh yeah?"

"Definitely." She pulled the zipper of her gray hooded sweatshirt up to her tanned collarbones.

Somewhere around noon, Julianne reached for the cement. As she stretched across the tiny bathroom, trying to wrap her fingers around the handle of the cement bucket and grab the wooden stirrer, the edge of her hoodie got caught on a loose piece of cabinet that hadn't been installed yet. She lost her balance and went tumbling into the bathtub, the cement from the stirrer splashing across Remi's new button-down, and one lone drop landing on his nose. The bucket teetered dangerously on the ledge for a moment before mercifully settling back in place.

Cement-splattered, Remi spun around, nearly as surprised to see Julianne sprawled out in the newly installed bathtub as she was to be there. "Hey, lady, you better watch where you're splashing that stuff!" Remi scolded in mock indignation.

"Or what?" Julianne shot back. "You're going to rap my knuckles with your big bad T-square?" She burst into hysterical laughter as Remi tried to put on his best "I mean business" face.

"You know," she managed to gasp between bouts of laughter, "it would be a lot easier to take you seriously if you didn't have cement on your nose." Remi groped around his face, trying to locate and remove the offending cement. "C'mere." Julianne reached a hand out to Remi and pulled him into the bathtub on top of her. She licked one finger like a child's grandmother in a shopping mall and started to scrub the cement off of his nose. Before Julianne could reach in for a second try, Remi caught her with a long kiss.

"I think I missed a spot," Julianne breathed between kisses, tenderly reaching toward the remaining cement speckled on Remi's nose.

"I think I can live with that," Remi murmured back, winding his hand under Julianne's tangle of curls and letting it rest on the warm nape of her neck. He pulled her face back to his again.

Julianne eased her lips apart, making room for Remi's mouth on hers. Every time they kissed she only wanted to kiss more, kiss longer, and memorize the feeling of their lips meshing against each other. Reflexively, she felt her entire body relax and sink into Remi's. She pressed her palms flat against his strong back and pulled herself even closer to him. He did the same.

The outline of his cheek and nose pressed under her ear made Julianne positively giddy. She leaned back and slid down along the bathtub's flat floor, bringing Remi along with her. She felt free and powerful and so ridiculously alive, in a way that nothing other than making art had ever sparked in her before.

"Stop!" Julianne giggled. "Did you hear something?"

"Probably just the guys upstairs making fun of us for a change." Remi shrugged before kissing her again. Before long, Julianne and Remi were too focused on making out to hear the bathroom door open.

Julianne heard a sickeningly familiar gasp. She froze under Remi, who took a few seconds to realize she'd stopped kissing him back. Julianne slowly sat up and pulled her hair out of her eyes. She thought she was hallucinating. Standing in front of the bathtub, slack-jawed in horror, her eyes filling with angry tears, was Chloe. Julianne zipped up her hoodie and leapt out of the bathtub in one motion.

"Chloe?! What are you doing here?" She was pretty sure her heart was beating louder than Randy's hammer upstairs. This was actually what it felt like the second before the whole world ended. Oh. My. God.

"Well, I'm not making out with my archenemy in a bathtub." Chloe was oddly matter-of-fact as she said it.

All of the color had drained from her face and her hazel eyes looked like dull coins. "The living room flooded. Badly. Dad's in New York and I need your help. I can't do it by myself."

Julianne looked at her robot sister and nodded dumbly. "Sure." She heard the word hanging in the air before she realized that she had said it.

Chloe looked from Julianne to Remi and back again. Then she stormed out, her hot pink galoshes squealing through the basement. Julianne began to run after her, then stopped mid-stride and turned to Remi. His eyes widened, and he started to reach a hand out to her. "I can't see you again," she heard herself say blankly before chasing Chloe out to the car.

For most of the ride home the sisters sat in tense, awkward silence. Finally, Julianne couldn't take it anymore. "Chloe, I'm so, so sor–" but Chloe dismissed her apology with a wave of her hand, restoring silence to the car. Julianne had never seen her sister like this before. She was terrified and completely overwhelmed with guilt.

Then it was like someone flipped Chloe's on switch. All of the color came rushing back into her face, along with a lot of extra red. She went ballistic.

"I can't believe you!" she bellowed at Julianne, before rapidly changing her mind and switching tactics. "No, I can't believe *him*!" She ran her hands through her hair like she was on the verge of ripping it out in clumps. She flailed, and if she hadn't been piloting a small car down a flooded highway, she probably would have started pacing. "It's not enough that he knocks me over at the first party of the summer," she continued. "It's not enough that he and his yuppie, tacky-ass parents move in and build the largest, ugliest house in the history of the universe. It's not enough that they're trying to kick my family out of the home we've owned since *before I was born* to make more room for their McMansion, but now he goes and screws around with my baby sister?! Is he evil? Is that his deal? Is he actually a malicious person who gets his kicks out of harming others?"

If Julianne hadn't been scared for her life, she would have made Chloe rewind all the way to "tacky-ass." In any other situation it would have been hysterical that the phrase had even crossed her sister's well-glossed lips. But she *was* scared for her life, so she just sat there, glued to the gray upholstery, stupefied as Chloe turned her rage away from Remi and back in Jules's direction. "And *you!*" she shrieked at her. "I don't think I can ever forgive you! How could you? How dare you? Julianne, if I can't trust my own sister, who can I trust? The Moores are trying to take our house away—they are actively trying to make us homeless so they can install a freakin' sauna—and you're practically sleeping with their son? At work? Jules, who *are* you? You've totally betrayed our family. What would Mom think of this?"

Julianne sat there silently, almost numb, staring out the rain-streaked windshield with tears streaming down her face. She couldn't think of anything to say in her own defense. Maybe Chloe was right. Maybe she was a traitor. She tried to quell the torrent of words spilling out of Chloe's mouth. "Chloe, I never meant . . . Remi's really—" she began.

Chloe cut her off before Julianne could figure out where her own thoughts were going. "Remi?!" she barked. "You trust him over me? Over Dad? Over every single solid thing we've seen happen this summer? Grow up, Jules—he's probably using you to find out how much it would take for us to just sell outright to his parents! He's probably a spy!"

It had never occurred to Julianne in all of her imaginary spy scenarios that she could be double-crossed. She felt cold all over. Remi was just using her. He had been spying on her for his father all along. Of course! How could she have been so stupid? Remi idolized his father. He was using Julianne to help his father make his architectural dreams come true. Jules forgot everything she had felt in that stupid bathtub, for the past month, and even the first time she had seen Remi at the bonfire party. It was like the anger accompanying Chloe's words automatically made them true. Julianne couldn't move. She sat in the passenger seat, tears silently staining her face until her dark curls hung limply against her cheekbones.

"I can't believe you would compromise our position like this!" Chloe continued. "Did you know that we might have to sell the house? Did you even realize that? I can't believe you would do this to us! As soon as Dad gets back to LA, you need to tell him about this, Julianne. If you don't, I will."

Julianne couldn't argue. She spent the rest of the car ride in the same stunned silence.

When Julianne and Chloe got home, Julianne ran right into the living room to assess the damage. At the very least, she could be helpful. All told, the flooding wasn't bad. The old ottoman was soaked through; it would need to be replaced. So would the rocking chair, but it had been slowly crumbling for years, anyway.

As Julianne scanned the room for additional damage, her heart caught in her chest. Last week when she'd given her mother's painting to Dad and Chloe, they'd propped it up against the grate in front of the fireplace, to get an idea of how it would look above the mantel. Sure enough, her painting–her mom's painting–that she'd worked so hard on all summer had been caught in the deluge. A border of about four inches of paint at the bottom of the canvas was totally distorted. She couldn't even tell it was paint, let alone a picture of their beach.

It was completely ruined. Everything was completely ruined.

Chapter Twenty–one

✦

For the next few days, Julianne walked around like a zombie. She called out sick from work, ignoring the obvious concern in Bill's voice. She just couldn't face Remi.

Chloe wouldn't talk to her or even look at her.

She'd never known Chloe to hate another living soul in her entire life, and she never in a million years would have thought that she'd be the first. Julianne could barely even sleep. Every time she closed her eyes, she had horrible nightmares about telling her father what she'd done. In one, he threw her out of the house, leaving her with nowhere to live but the beach—which wasn't really an option, because the Moores had paved over the entire thing and built an amusement park. In another, Dad made Jules walk down to her mother's grave to apologize in person for betraying her memory, only to find the epitaph had been changed to read, "I don't forgive you."

The flood damage in the living room was so intense that Julianne wasn't sure how to tackle it, so she'd decided to start by cleaning the rest of the house first. As Julianne pedaled her bike toward Palisades Hardware for cleaning supplies, she looked at the clear sky and sparkling beaches and couldn't believe that this was just a pocket in between miserable storms. The fronds of the palm trees were a lush green, and the beach looked smooth as stone. She pulled up in front of the store, checked her pocket for her shopping list, and pushed down her kickstand. Locking her bike, she headed inside.

Julianne was standing near the front of the store, trying to figure out how much of what she needed would fit in her bike basket and her backpack, when she heard her name. Looking up, she saw Liz Moss, a girl from school who'd sat behind her in calculus last year.

"Julianne! How are you?" Liz asked with a hug. "You look upset. Are you okay?"

Julianne made a concerted effort to perk up. "Yeah, I'm okay. Just a little bit stressed. The storm hit us pretty hard. The entire living room is flooded and my dad's out of town, so I've got lots to do." Julianne gestured at the aisles of the store. "How has your summer been?"

"Oh, yuck. Sorry about your living room. My summer has been good." Liz's shaggy, blond hair bounced around her face. "I've been lifeguarding—the usual. It's been really nice. But I promised my mom I'd help her stain the deck today, so here I am."

"Well, have fun. It was great running into you." Julianne gave Liz a hug goodbye.

"Yeah, good luck with the flooding stuff," Liz said as she turned to go. "But I wouldn't worry too much about it, Jules—if worse comes to worst, you can always move into that glass castle thing that's growing next to your house!" Liz giggled and waved as she walked off to find her mother. Julianne sighed and headed in the opposite direction.

The last few days, she'd been getting out of bed in the middle of the night, cleaning and dusting and straightening the house. She was fixing the things she knew how to fix before Dad got home and everything else fell apart again.

✦ ✦ ✦

When she got home from the hardware store, she beat out the rugs over the deck railing and sorted the wrapping paper in the living room drawer by color. Julianne couldn't sit still, but she didn't have any idea what to do with herself, either.

She was shocked that she could feel this lousy. She couldn't eat. She couldn't sleep. She had completely destroyed everyone she loved. And, to top it all off, her mother's painting was totally ruined. The paint had twisted into grotesque lumps of oil and plastic; even the canvas underneath had warped. She wouldn't even know where to begin to repaint it. It had been so hard the first time, Julianne couldn't imagine trying to reconstruct it now—what with most of the summer light gone, along with the view of the beach that had informed it in the first place, not to mention her ability to see anything beautiful in the world at all. She had somehow managed to lose every single thing she cared about. Julianne moved through the living room, trying to separate out cushions that were ruined from ones that were still usable. She had been planning on taking the now saggy, waterlogged ottoman out back to dry a bit before she left it on the curb, but it had started pouring again right after she returned from the hardware store. She set up fans to dry out the rest of the soggy furniture and mopped up the few puddles that had collected along the floor moldings when the rain picked up again. Frustrated at how little progress she was making, she sat on the window seat, looking out on the angry gray waves, her forehead pressed against the cold glass and her ruined painting sitting dejectedly at her feet.

Julianne felt the chill of the dampening windowpane

sink into her forehead and settle behind her eyes. As the cold seared its way into her brain, she tried to see the ocean through the foggy window. In the periphery of her vision, she saw palm trees bending over themselves. It looked to her like they were trying not to break in two. Julianne knew the feeling. She thought of all the times during the summer that she'd felt like everything was a mess and she just felt stupid. Deeply, profoundly stupid. She wished she had appreciated how lucky she was before it all fell apart. Even though she was terrified that her family would lose their house, there had at least been something comforting to fall back on. Chloe had been her best friend. Dad had been tirelessly optimistic. She'd been caught up in the whirlwind thrill of loving Remi. If nothing else, she'd had things to work toward. Toward finishing her painting, toward saving the house, toward finding a way to be with Remi. Now there was nothing to run to. Chloe couldn't even look at her without turning eggplant purple, and Dad would undoubtedly feel the same way when he got back. She'd misjudged Remi, and now the Moores were going to take her home. And, of course, there was the fact that her heart had been torn into millions of microscopic pieces.

Julianne pushed herself up off the cushions and paced through the musty living room, her footsteps keeping time with the raindrops outside the window. She was moving so quickly that when she looked down, she saw nothing but a brightly colored trail of hot pink toenail polish. Swiping her tears away wildly, Julianne told herself, *I will not cry. Not now.* She gazed down at her pajamas, a black sleeveless T-shirt and drawstring pants printed with cartoon sushi rolls, and almost didn't recognize them. Julianne felt strangely separate from the body they were hanging off of.

Outside, the rain was still pouring down in bucket loads and the wind was shrieking, but Julianne didn't care. She couldn't sit around with her racing thoughts for one second longer or something was going to snap. *I just need to do something,* she told herself. She sprinted up the stairs and made a beeline for her bedroom. Julianne threw on her grubbiest painting clothes. Then, without looking back, she rushed out of her room and bolted down the stairs, barefoot.

She threw herself into cleaning the house from top to bottom, keeping herself focused on the task at hand. Before she knew it, she was sliding around on the wood floors, rags tied to her knees and feet like one of the orphans in *Annie.* She polished all of the candlesticks and the silver coffee percolator that probably hadn't shined since her parents got them as wedding presents. She even called to rent a steam cleaner for the water stains on the living room rug. Then she did all of her laundry.

Julianne stayed up all night, cleaning and scrubbing,

and when the morning sun shone through the back windows, it was undeniable how beautiful her home was. It was bright and open, yet still cozy. When she scrubbed the windows of the balcony attached to her bedroom, she was literally breathless at the streaks of orange, pink, and lavender reflecting off the ocean as the sun was rising. From the bay window off of Julianne's balcony, the beach went on forever—at least when she had her back to the Moores' glass house—and the ocean went even farther. She understood exactly why her mother had known this house would be their home the first time she saw it.

As she tiptoed through the house, Julianne had the strangest feeling that her mom was walking with her. Every beam of sunlight—bouncing from one surface Julianne had scrubbed to another—seemed to have her mother all over it. Julianne crept into the living room and curled up on the couch, watching as morning spread across the beach. She felt quiet and peaceful for the first time all week.

Chapter Twenty-two

✦

Julianne smoothed the fringe around the edge of the pillow she was clutching and tried to take deep, cleansing breaths. She could hear her father downstairs and knew it was time to face the music. Chloe was finishing up her shift at the hospital, so Julianne figured it was a good time to throw herself on her father's mercy, admit that she was a horrible person and a disgrace to the family, and get disowned. This way, if things went really badly, she could still be out of the house and on her way to join a circus troupe by dinnertime.

Her father was moving his bags from the foyer into his studio, rifling through some papers, when Julianne stuck her head into the room. Her heart was pounding at what could not be a healthy rate, and she was pretty sure that her knees had stopped working. Their cozy little foyer suddenly seemed menacing and dark. She took a deep breath, counted to ten (which might have been more like a count to fifty), and forced her legs to move forward.

"Hi, Dad. Welcome back. Um, can I talk to you for a second?" Julianne tried to sound upbeat as she slid down onto one of the huge cushions on the window seat, hoping to lose herself in the crevices. "I'm so sorry, Dad, but I have some things I need to tell you." Mr. Kahn sat next to his youngest daughter.

"What's wrong, sweetie? Are you okay?" Dad patted Julianne's back as she took another deep breath and tried not to cry. He looked so kind and worried that Julianne felt like her heart might break all over again. She tried to steady herself for the words that had to come next. Then she took another deep breath and pulled her mop of hair up off of her neck.

Julianne began slowly. "Um, Dad, while you were gone . . ." She paused and looked into her father's patient green eyes and felt her nerve begin to waver. "While you were gone, the living room flooded. Everything is mildewed."

Her father's eyes moved furtively around the room, from the window seat to the bookshelves and back. "The place does look a little worse for wear," he noted. "But it doesn't even smell like mildew in here."

Julianne felt her cheeks flush with guilt. "I steam cleaned." She kept her eyes on the hem of her linen patchwork skirt.

"Jules, sweetie, I sense that you're not telling me the whole story. Did you and Chloe throw some crazy party while I was gone?" Dad's brow creased and he cocked his head toward his daughter.

Julianne shook her head mutely, her eyes glued to the floor.

Dad continued, "Because I seem to remember another weekend not so long ago when I returned to find there'd been a Slip 'n' Slide–related mishap in the living room." His voice trailed off.

"That was not a party!" Julianne blurted out. "That was performance art!" To this day, Dad had never made his daughters replace any of the vases broken during that ill-fated event, out of respect for their artistic vision. Julianne felt a small smile creeping onto her face and didn't try to hold it back. Smiling felt good after a week of being frozen in grief. A few tentative giggles welled up in her throat and escaped her lips.

Then, all of a sudden, the floodgates opened and all of the desperation, guilt, and sadness that Julianne had been pushing down came rushing out of her in a jumble.

"I didn't mean to betray the family, Dad!"

"Julianne, what are you talking about? Don't be silly! You could never betray us." Dad's voice was comforting, but Julianne also heard confusion in it. She heard a clicking noise beyond the living room, but she was too focused on her confession to investigate further.

"No, really, I did. I never meant to, but I did!" Julianne continued.

"Jules, I'm not sure I know what you're talking about, but I do know that you could never *betray* us. I know how much you love your sister and me." The kindness in Dad's voice sent Julianne over the edge. In between sobs and gasps, the entire story of her summer romance came pouring out.

"I'm so sorry, Dad," she finished in a great rush of tears. "I wish I could take it all back. I wish I could undo all of it. I'm sorry for betraying the family and for betraying Mom's memory and for everything. I'm sorry I fell in love with Remi. I didn't mean to–I couldn't help it. It just happened. And I'm sorry. I'm so, so sorry." Her blue eyes were drowning with tears as she peered up into her father's face waiting for the worst.

Dad smiled and Julianne let out a long breath–it was her first exhale all week that hadn't been soaked in sobs. "I wish I could forgive you, kiddo, but I can't."

Julianne swallowed and felt her heart sink to her feet.

"I can't forgive someone who doesn't have anything to be sorry for. You haven't done anything wrong." Dad spoke with a quiet resolution. He looked over his daughter's shoulder, out onto the mangled beach.

Julianne's heart zoomed back into place and threat-ened to tear right through her chest.

"You're not angry?" She said it slowly, disbelievingly.

"Julianne, I don't have anything to be angry about. Do I wish that you didn't hide things from me? Of course. Every parent wishes that. Do I wish you felt com-fortable enough to tell me that you were feeling pres-sured and conflicted? You know that I do. But you're old enough to make your own decisions about the kind of support you need from your family." Dad's voice remained calm, almost pleasant, as he spoke.

Julianne couldn't help but wonder if maybe her father hadn't completely understood her confession. She had practically been sleeping with the enemy—well, not *sleeping with* the enemy, but definitely making out with the enemy—for weeks, and he wasn't even batting an eyelash.

As soon as Julianne opened her mouth, she knew she would regret it, but she just had to ask, "But after every-thing the Moores have done to you—to us—you're not angry?" She let her voice trail off, slightly afraid of what was coming next.

Her dad paused, clearly weighing his words before sighing and crossing his arms in front of his chest. "Look. What the Moores are doing—it's terrible. It's greedy, it's wasteful, and it's unkind. There's no doubt that these folks play dirty, and there's no doubt that I disagree—I can't stress enough how *strongly*—with what they want to do with our property. But this kid isn't the one doing it. His parents are."

"But he's not even trying to stop them!" Julianne was surprised at how easily she moved to attack Remi.

"Maybe he is, maybe he isn't. I don't know. That's not my concern. But Julianne, this Remi isn't his parents. He's not his family. He's not the one doing this." Dad's voice remained clear and slow, like he was doing a public service announcement. "Imagine if the situation were turned on its ear, okay? Let's say that you really wanted us to sell the house . . ."

"But . . ." Julianne tried to cut in, but her father continued with his example, drowning out her feeble protests.

"It's just an example, okay? Stick with me, here. Let's say that you really wanted us to sell the house, but Chloe and I didn't agree." He looked at Julianne for an indication that she was following the same train of thought.

"Okay . . ." Julianne conceded hesitantly.

"If Chloe and I said to you, 'Julianne, we know you don't agree with what we want, but, as a member of our family, we really need your support in not selling the house,' would you support us?" Dad asked quietly.

"Of course I would. You're my family." Julianne was a little bit surprised her father would ask something so obvious.

"Then why is it so impossible to think that this boy would do the same thing for his family?" Dad pressed gently.

Blood rushed to Julianne's face. Her head was suddenly swirling with frustration and confusion, thoughts tripping over each other like clowns in a mad rush to get out of their tiny car. "Why are you defending him?"

Dad took a few moments' pause, and Julianne's stomach started back up with its familiar twisting. "I'm not defending him, Jules—I don't even know him. But it's obvious that he's pretty important to you . . ."

Julianne looked down at her feet. The radiant pink polish she had borrowed from Chloe weeks ago was starting to chip.

"And you should certainly know what it feels like to want to support and stand up for your family. It's what you've always done for us." Dad reached out and tousled Julianne's hair before getting up and heading for the kitchen, leaving her to sort out her tangled thoughts by herself.

"You know, I had a feeling something was going on all summer." Dad stopped and turned back toward Jules, his hazel eyes twinkling.

"How?" Julianne's head snapped around toward her father, her mouth agape.

"You were never around. Even when you weren't working with Bill or painting, I practically never saw you. And you know, I don't think Remi's parents had seen much of him, as I recall from some extremely awkward small talk." Julianne blushed. "It's really okay, honey," her father continued offhandedly. "Believe it or not, I was in love once too."

Julianne leapt off the window seat and followed her father toward the kitchen.

"Between you and me, your grandfather wasn't so wild about his 'hippie son-in-law' when your mom and I first got together." Her dad opened the refrigerator and reached for a small blue Tupperware container of sprouts and some pita bread.

"What happened?" Julianne asked eagerly.

"Nothing, really. These things take time. All you can do is try to listen closely and follow what your heart is telling you. Can you pass me the hummus, sweetie?" Julianne ducked down, plucked the container of hummus from the bottom shelf of the fridge, and tossed it out to her father. "You're a good egg, Julianne Kahn, and I'm proud of you always." Dad held his arms out for a hug, and Julianne curled up against his broad chest and let herself be held. She was beyond happy.

Just then, Julianne and Dad heard the quiet click of heels coming in from the hallway, and Chloe walked into the kitchen. Her hazel eyes were cast toward the floor.

Julianne looked up, the warmth and security of her father's hug draining out of her as cold damp fear about being in the same room with Chloe trickled in. She swallowed hard and tried to brace herself for Chloe's anger. But it never came. Julianne had never seen her sister look so sheepish. Knowing that a convincing poker face was not one of Chloe's many talents, Julianne could only assume she'd been listening. She wanted to laugh. Subtlety was never one of her sister's strengths.

Chloe was shaking ever so slightly, and her coffee-colored hair was staticky around the crown of her head—Julianne knew that when Chloe was nervous she ran her fingers through her hair compulsively. It looked like Chloe had been nervous for quite a while.

"Um, hi." Chloe's voice was quiet and tentative. "Welcome home, Dad."

Dad smiled benevolently in the direction of his older daughter.

Chloe cleared her throat and smoothed her wrinkled scrub shirt. "Hey, Jules."

"Hey." Julianne really didn't know what to say next. A part of her wanted to run over and throw her arms around her sister. Another part of her wanted to hit Chloe in the face with a pie. She also considered hopping in the sisters' shared hybrid and not looking back until she'd safely crossed the state border.

"Um, I was sort of listening out there and I have a few things I'd like to say." Chloe's voice pulled Julianne from her imagined escape back into the warm kitchen.

Julianne found her own voice hiding in the back of her throat and piped up. "Listen, Chloe, I know that you're angry at me right now. I know that I let you down, and I know that I should have been honest with you, but if you give me a chance to explain—"

"I don't want an explanation from you, Julianne." Chloe's voice had a note of finality to it that terrified Jules.

"Chloe, really, just hear me out." She didn't want to plead with her sister, but she needed Chloe to understand her—to forgive her—the way Dad had.

"No, Jules. I don't need to. I really don't." Chloe's tone left little room for discussion and it stopped Jules dead in her tracks. "You didn't do anything wrong."

Julianne was stunned. After all the silence and the slamming doors and the icy glares, now Chloe was holding out the proverbial olive branch? As much as Julianne had wanted this, hoped for it, daydreamed about it over the last week, she honestly hadn't expected it to happen. She knew she was staring at her sister as though Chloe had grown an extra head, but she could not find a single word to say in response.

Chloe continued resolutely. "I'm really sorry for all of the horrible things I said. Well, except the things about the Moores' house. I totally meant all of those. And it felt really good to say them, too." A grin flickered across Chloe's lips, and she and Julianne both let out a nervous laugh. "But about you and about Remi—I'm sorry. I had no right to say any of that, and it was wrong. I was wrong."

Julianne watched Chloe's face as she spoke. Her chin was set in determination. Her eyes were nearly transparent in their intensity, and as she spoke, it was as if Chloe relaxed into the truth of her words. Her shoulders dropped as the tension drained out of them.

"You didn't betray us. I'm sorry for saying that. I'm sorry for thinking it. I don't know where that came from and it was a whole lot of melodramatic guilt to throw at you. You were just trying to be true to yourself. And I've always loved that about you." Chloe made her way down the kitchen counter until she was standing next to Jules and her father and let herself be swept into the family hug. "I am so sorry. I didn't realize how irrational and cruel I was being," Chloe continued, both Jules's and Dad's arms wrapped around her. "I guess the scientific black-or-white thing isn't always the best way to approach emotional questions."

Julianne practically burst with relief. "Well, if we're being fair, I don't think sneaking around the way I did was the best choice I've ever made. I guess I was just so afraid of what you would think that it never occurred to me to actually level with you."

Chloe laughed. "Okay, this is getting a little too after-school special, even for me. I'm seriously going to start crying if we don't ratchet down the heart-to-heart factor a little bit here."

"Ooooh noooo," Julianne warned. "I'm not done with you yet." She pitched her voice up into a dramatic falsetto. "Oh, Chloe, how can you ever forgive me? You're my best friend in the world—I would be lost without you. Chloe, just tell me what to do to make it up to you . . . anything." Julianne widened her eyes earnestly, and batted her long eyelashes at her sister.

Chloe rolled her eyes. "Cue the made-for-TV music."

Julianne sighed dramatically. "*Fiiine.* I guess you'll never know the deeply heartfelt lessons I've learned from this whole growing process."

Chloe smiled. "You know, I think I've got some ideas." The look on her face said she completely understood.

Dad pulled the girls in close, and they all stared out over the ocean. They just stood there, close to one another.

"I really am sorry about what happened with your painting," Chloe said seriously. "I know how hard you worked on it. And how much it meant to you to do that for Mom."

Julianne shrugged, but she felt a lump forming at the back of her throat. "I just wanted to keep a little tiny piece of her alive, I guess."

Dad spoke gently. "You know, girls, we don't need a painting, or this house, or this beach to know what home feels like. Don't you worry about Mom's memory. No matter where we are, she'll be with us."

Julianne felt her mouth stretching into a grin, her eyes brimming with happy tears.

Chapter Twenty-three

✦

Julianne was running down the beach at full speed, the sand flying under her sneakers, the sun racing to keep up with her. Since the flooding had mauled her painting, she had been running on the beach each day to clear her head. She usually didn't run much outside of cross-country season, and she was pleasantly surprised by how much she enjoyed it. Her iPod was strapped to her arm with an athletic strap, and despite being pulled back with a blue stretchy headband, a handful of loose curls stuck to her neck. She could feel the music propelling her down the beach. She ran through Kelly Clarkson, Fergie, Beyoncé, and Missy Elliott, but when Gwen Stefani snuck into the shuffle, she felt herself launching ahead double-time over the uneven ground. Julianne briefly thought of running along the waterline where the waves and shifting tides had made the sand wet and smooth and packed flat, but decided against it. If she was going to run on the beach, she was going for the biggest challenge she could handle.

Since her talk with Dad and Chloe, life in the Kahn household had been warm, fun, and relatively uneventful once again—if somewhat bittersweet. Julianne and Chloe were closer than they'd ever been, but Julianne knew that their renewed bond was underscored by a sense of loss.

As she headed back down the beach for home, Julianne's runner's high was tainted by the realization that she'd have to run past the Moores' place on her way home. The Moore property was expanding so rapidly that it would have been almost impossible to avoid it. Julianne took a deep breath, promising herself yet again that running past the massive construction site in no way compromised the campaign of avoidance she'd launched against Remi over the past weeks.

After talking about it a lot with Dad and Chloe, Julianne had more or less acknowledged that Remi was an innocent bystander in his family's expansion campaign, but she still couldn't bring herself to talk to him. Fair or not, he was still tangled up in the messy web of the summer's hurt and loss, and Julianne wasn't ready to untangle that part just yet. She had too much else to deal with. She shifted her eyes away from the looming construction and focused instead on the gleaming, turquoise water. The ocean looked like an exact replica of Julianne's painting, giving her a familiar pang of pride and loss. As Julianne stretched her long legs into a comfortable gait, she ran with her head slightly turned. She just couldn't keep her eyes off the water. It felt a little too much like a sitcom setup. *At any moment,* Julianne thought, *I'll probably get bonked on the forehead by a stray Frisbee, or I'll collide with another runner who had his eyes on the water, too.* She was still laughing at her own imagination when the playlist shuffled to "SexyBack." Julianne quickened her stride and let Justin steer her back toward home.

Arriving on the porch, her sound track still blaring in her ears, Julianne leaned down to stretch her calves before taking off her running shoes. Taking a little hop forward, she pulled her right heel behind her back and held it with her left hand. Every time she came back from a run, Julianne looked up at her bedroom balcony and promised herself that this wouldn't be the last time she'd dash over the sand and return to the house she loved. She sighed and finished her stretch before kicking off her sneakers onto the porch and heading inside.

She padded into her bedroom in her white ankle socks with green and yellow pom-poms. When Julianne had first bought the socks, Chloe had laughed that they'd ruin her athletic cred. Julianne paused in front of her mirror, rolling her eyes at her red, sweaty face and her soggy curls. She turned to Chloe, who was sprawled out on Julianne's bed reading *Us Weekly*.

"I look like Miss Piggy," Julianne declared.

"No you don't. You look sporty. Well, except for the socks." Chloe giggled. Humming "Hollaback Girl" quietly to herself, Julianne headed over to her desk and plunked herself down in front of her computer. She was trying to decide between the online crossword and Perez Hilton when the blinking lights of her cell phone caught her eye. Julianne reached across her round Jackson Pollock mouse pad to grab her phone off the desk, but Chloe darted over from across the room and beat her to it.

"Hmm. I wonder who it could possibly be?" Chloe queried in a singsong voice. She looked at the blinking display, then passed the phone to Jules before returning to the *Us Weekly* on the bed.

Julianne let a few minutes pass and then reluctantly scrolled through her missed call log. 9:45 a.m.–Remi Moore. 10:56 a.m.–Remi Moore. 11:32 a.m.–Remi Moore. 12:19 p.m.–Remi Moore. She pitched the phone across the room, thankfully hitting an overstuffed pillow on her bed, rather than Chloe. She rubbed her hands roughly over her face, looking the very picture of lovelorn angst. *Why won't he stop calling? What part of "I*

Hailey Abbott

can't see you again" can't he accept? How will I ever superglue my heart back together if Remi won't leave me alone with the pieces? A tiny nagging voice in the back of Julianne's brain occasionally reminded her that if Remi *did* finally stop calling and texting fifteen times a day, she'd be devastated. Beyond devastated. But Julianne couldn't focus on her messy feelings for Remi right now—there was too much else left up in the air. She pushed herself up from the desk chair and crossed the room to her bed, completely ignoring Chloe, who was still settled in with her magazine. She picked up a stray pillow in a flowered pillowcase and tossed it on top of the cell phone. Then she strode out of the room toward a well-deserved shower, leaving Chloe exactly where she'd found her.

Julianne emerged from the shower forty-five minutes—and three encores of "Irreplaceable"—later, refreshed and ready to take on the rest of her afternoon. She slipped on a pair of skinny jeans, a white tank top trimmed in hot pink lace—the result of a recent shopping trip with Chloe—and her cute, turquoise slip-ons. She futzed with the clasp of a necklace featuring a hammered metal star that she'd made in lapidary club during sophomore year. Julianne took a cursory glance in the mirror before sliding her oversize sunglasses up the bridge of her nose. The she grabbed her digital camera—complete with its new zoom lens, thanks to a summer of gainful employment—and headed out of her bedroom.

As she walked past Chloe's room, she heard her sister call, "Jules, is that you?"

Jules walked in and plopped herself facedown on Chloe's bed, next to Chloe's hefty stack of surgery guides and diagrams. *No wonder she comes to my room to read* Us Weekly, Julianne thought.

"So," Chloe said authoritatively. "Does he always call you seventeen times a day?"

Julianne cast her eyes toward the floor. "On average."

"He really likes you, Jules," Chloe declared, her voice softer. "I mean, he really, really likes you."

"I know," Julianne admitted.

"Then why are you sitting around the house moping with me all the time?" Chloe asked, a smile crossing her face. "Go out there and get that boy back. Before he actually starts believing that you want nothing to do with him."

"But—" Julianne began to protest.

"But nothing. You deserve to be happy. So go. Go and be happy with your boyfriend." Chloe smiled and swatted Julianne's arm. "I mean it—leave. I have a lot of celebrity gossip to catch up on." Chloe slipped a copy of *People* out of her *Guide to Cardiothoracic Surgery* and opened it with a satisfied sigh. All Julianne could do was walk out of Chloe's room, camera firmly in hand.

Moments later, Julianne found herself stalking around the side of the house like an incredibly obvious cat burglar. Just two months earlier, this kind of "casing the perimeter" would have meant that Jules was on the prowl with her super-spy hat on. Today it meant something entirely different to Julianne, though. Her digital camera was hanging from the '60s-inspired strap around her neck, dangling at the ready. She was determined to photograph every angle, crevice, and shadow of the Kahn house before the Moores forced them out.

Even if she, Dad, and Chloe couldn't hold on to their physical house, she was determined to create a photographic history of of it. She hadn't decided whether she would frame each shot individually or piece them together in a mural. Dad had promised her free rein over the family room in their next house and, even though Chloe pointed out that it was *slightly* morbid, Julianne planned to erect a fitting tribute to their life-long home.

The new school year was rapidly approaching, and Julianne was still trying to wrap her brain around all that had transpired this summer. So much had happened over the last three months that it seemed crazy to Julianne that she was about to just slide back into another September at Palisades High School—the September of her senior year. She was trying to re-acclimate her brain to academic life by reciting the names and capitals of all fifty states, while she snapped her pictures of the house. Then, when she stopped to adjust the light meter on her camera to catch some shadows poking up from the sea grass that surrounded the house, something occurred to her. Despite all the end-of-summer stress, at this exact moment, she was at peace. The sun was at her back. Her nose was filled with the salty air of an August afternoon in Southern California, and she was looking at her crazy life through the lens of a camera.

Even with the crushing loss of her home looming before her, Julianne was still able to create art. It was as easy as looking at life through her own eyes and being completely honest with her vision. Last week she'd taken three rolls of film—one black and white, one sepia toned, and one in eye-popping color—of the ocean view from the beach behind her house. It was the same landscape she had struggled to capture all summer. But viewed through the lens of her camera, the scene came together effortlessly.

Julianne worked her way methodically around the house, snapping pictures for the next three hours. She wanted to remember what the house looked like at every moment of every day—with every change of light. She was also determined not to let her last weeks in the house be a blur of crying and exhaustion. She planned to celebrate life in their little beach home until the Moores and their lawyers dragged her out the front door kicking, screaming, and snapping pictures of the whole mess.

Julianne was relieved to have wrapped everything up with her job at the site. Her courtyard mural had turned out fabulously, and she was thrilled to have such a great new piece to add to her portfolio. It was also a relief not to have to deal with questions from the guys on the crew about her and Remi.

As the sun slipped down behind the ocean, the sky did its slow-motion fade from brilliant navy blue to the cobalt-gray hybrid of a late summer night. Julianne walked down to the beachfront, her camera tapping against her sternum in time with her heartbeat.

Floating in the haze of her thoughts about her photography, the house, and the arrival of fall, Julianne was only half-aware that she was heading onto the Moores' property. Beyond the jurisdiction of the orange trespassing signs, Julianne's immediate instinct was to plop down on the sand at the bottom of the construction dunes. She snuggled down at the base of the dune and pulled her legs up in front of her.

You can miss him—it's okay to miss him, Julianne told herself. She pulled her legs in close to her chest—careful not to disturb her camera—and looked out onto the empty ocean. After a few minutes of listening to the echo of the crashing waves, Julianne realized she was shivering slightly. She stood up, dusted the sand off the bottom of her jeans, and readied herself to head home. She had only gone two steps toward her house when she saw light coming from one of the stark, minimalist rooms of the Moores' glass house. Julianne peered up the hill and saw Remi backlit against the August night.

Even from her perch frozen at the bottom of the dune, Julianne could tell that Remi was arguing with someone. A moment more of peering into the massive glass mansion revealed the designer-suit-clad silhouette of Remi's father. Remi's face was twisted into a determined grimace, and he was gesticulating wildly with what appeared to be a roll of paper. His father's arms were crossed tightly over his double-breasted suit and tie. Julianne instantly remembered that Remi had told her his father only wore imported silk ties, and she rolled her eyes in spite of herself. Remi kept pointing to the paper tube in his hand, the very picture of an agitated, passionate fighter.

Julianne squinted. *What the hell? Are they actually fighting over wallpaper samples?* She didn't want to stick around to find out. Clearly, despite his calls and text messages, Remi's life was complicated enough without her. She shot a last departing look up the dunes at the feuding Moores before turning around. Then she walked back down the beach toward home, humming mournfully to herself the entire way.

Chapter Twenty-four

✦

The next day, Julianne and Chloe were sitting in the living room reading while their father worked in his studio. Dangling one leg over the side of an over-stuffed armchair, Julianne asked Chloe, "So, wait, where does he go to school?"

Chloe popped a pale green grape into her mouth before answering. "Stanford."

"And what's his name again?" Julianne pressed.

"Aaron." Chloe tossed another grape into the air and caught it in her mouth.

"And you met him on rotation at work?" After her own dating drama, Julianne found herself relishing Chloe's postdate recap.

"Yep. He's premed, too, but he's going to be a

junior." Chloe's cheeks were glowing a radiant pink. Her date two days ago had been such a success that Julianne thoroughly enjoyed hearing Chloe repeat all the details. She loved the way her sister's face glowed when she was this happy.

"And he took you out for Greek food?" Julianne continued.

"Yup. Definite points for that," Chloe chirped. "I am getting sick to death of first dates with checkered tablecloths and drippy candles. So overplayed." She giggled.

Julianne rolled her eyes playfully. "Okay, final question, but this one is the ultimate test: Did he ever, at any point in the evening, use the word 'chicks' or the delightful phrase 'smart for a girl' in any context?"

Chloe shut her eyes and let out a dramatic shudder at Julianne's reference to her disastrous first/last date with Michael at the beginning of the summer. The sisters laughed wickedly at the memory. "No and no!" Chloe declared victoriously. "There was absolutely no chauvinistic ickiness whatsoever. He was a complete and total rock star."

Julianne arched one eyebrow to let Chloe know that she was appropriately impressed. "Well, then, ladies and gents, I think we have a winner!"

"I hope so," Chloe remarked. "Have you given any thought to art school applications yet?"

"Not so much," Julianne admitted. "Although I was

thinking that the courtyard mural I did this summer might give me an edge. Not many people do outdoor art."

"And don't forget the pictures of our house! The sepia ones you took have 'professional artist' written all over them," Chloe added excitedly.

"Well, I'll clearly know who to call when I need a manager."

"I thought you'd never ask," Chloe shot back gleefully. "Do you want to hear my short-term educational plan for you, or the five-year business plan?" Just as Chloe was opening her mouth to share her (inevitably alphabetized and color-coded) strategies with her sister, the doorbell rang.

"Ooh, saved by the bell! You got lucky this time, Jules." Chloe jumped up and ran to the door.

Julianne heard her sister scamper into the hallway and throw open the door without even pausing to look out the peephole. She heard the opening whoosh, but then nothing else. After a few seconds of total silence, Julianne ambled over to her sister and was struck dumb. Standing on the stoop were Mr. and Mrs. Moore, dressed to the nines. At their side, Remi bounced slightly, like a runner getting ready to burst from the starting block.

Inches behind Julianne and her sister, their father wandered into the kitchen. Julianne could only assume that his jaw had dropped at the sight of their visitors as well. She wondered for a second why the still-silent Moores looked as shocked to find themselves on the Kahns' front steps as the Kahns were to see them there. *Hadn't they had a few minutes to get used to the idea on their walk over?* Julianne thought huffily. *While we, on the other hand, were totally blindsided!*

After an utterly awkward moment of Kahns staring at Moores and Moores staring at Kahns in complete and total silence, all attention shifted to Remi. While his parents sulked in the doorway, he rushed past Chloe, nearly knocking her down again, on his way into the Kahns' living room. He was carrying a large poster tube in one hand. Julianne recognized it as the mystery roll of paper from the little show she'd witnessed through the Moores' window the previous night. Now, standing this close to it, she was a little disappointed in herself for not recognizing blueprints when she saw them. Did these people actually think they could walk into her home with plans for remodeling?

"Remington! Come back here!" Mr. Moore snapped. He turned to Chloe, mainly because she was directly in front of him and said, "I apologize for my son's rash behavior."

"It's fine," Chloe said slowly. "*Your son* is always welcome here." Her voice was icy. "We have no problem at all with him."

Remi's words came rushing out, rapid fire. "Listen, Julianne, I know you said you never wanted to see me again, but please hear me out. Mr. Kahn, Chloe, I know we're the last people in the world you want in your living room but I promise you, this will only take five minutes of your time. Mom and Dad—I'm your son. We share DNA. You're stuck with me. So just try to pretend that you wouldn't rather be having a root canal." He took a deep breath as everyone gathered around him with varying degrees of caution. He popped open the lid of the poster tube and started to unroll large sheets of paper onto the Kahns' living room table.

Standing across the room, Julianne felt her hands shaking. She glanced on either side of her—at her father and Chloe—and knew that she wasn't alone in her anxiety. She cleared her throat, struggling to make words emerge from the dry, scared place between her heart and her mouth. "Um, what . . . what are you doing here?"

"I have an idea!" Remi burst out. Then he looked up from his pile of papers and blushed in Julianne's general direction. Julianne assumed Remi had noticed his father's stony-faced grimace, because he now spoke in his best "project manager" voice. "I'm here to make a . . ." He faltered. "I'm here to make an official business presentation. I think you may be, uh, very interested in the schematic I've worked up for this afternoon."

Julianne feared her heart was threatening to pound

out of her chest, with her stomach in hot pursuit. Instinctively, she reached for Chloe's hand and was relieved to feel her sister squeeze back. A few feet away, tiny beads of sweat were forming on their father's forehead.

Remi seemed to have gotten his second wind. Crouched on the living room floor, hunched over his pile of papers, he was busily sorting and shuffling and occasionally clearing his throat. Finally, after what felt like years, Remi scooped up some blueprints, transferred them to the coffee table, and turned to his father with shaking hands.

"Dad, I know that you've spent a long time, and a lot of money drawing up the plans for your house." Remi's voice had gained the tiniest edge of confidence.

Remi's father nodded severely. "You're absolutely right. This project has been years of work in the making. Years."

Remi pressed on before his father could elaborate. "But, bearing all those things in mind, I have something I'd really like you to consider." Remi took another deep breath and smoothed his blueprints out across the table. "I've been working with my boss at Dawson and Dawson on this all summer, and I think it could really work."

The room was completely silent as everyone held their breath, watching Mr. Moore lumber forward to leer down over the blueprints. Julianne could hear Remi gulping down air, but she couldn't look at him. "It's an alternative schematic for the new wing," Remi continued. "Dad, I know it's not your original plan, but I think you'll find it interesting. And it's totally eco-friendly. It would be groundbreaking—in a completely different way." He passed the blueprints over his shoulder to his father, who had gone from looking annoyed to downright shocked. Remi's mother took a few tentative steps forward to stand with her husband and glance over the blueprints. She stepped across the rug like she was trying to wipe something distasteful off of her shoe.

"I know it strays from your original vision, Dad," Remi pressed on. "But I think it's still viable. Living on this beach is a dream you share with a lot of people—I know it was a dream for Mrs. Kahn, too. I, um, I think we have that in common. We all deserve to build our dreams with our families, and no one should be able to take that away from us." He paused, shyly looking over at his father. "Maybe, this way, we can all have our dream houses."

Mrs. Moore raised her aristocratic—if slightly Botox-ed—chin toward her husband and then gestured back toward Remi's new blueprint. After what seemed like a lifetime, she said, "I, for one, think this is lovely." Mr. Moore slipped his hand around his wife's waist and clapped his son on the shoulder.

Nodding toward the blueprints, he said, "Well, Remington, the way you've worked solar panels in with the existing glass is very impressive. And turning that wing inward to create a contained beach garden that will be visible from the gym is a solid innovation." He paused, and when he spoke again, his tone was a little bit softer. "I'm impressed with the refinement in your design, son. The sustainable fixtures are going to save me quite a bit of money."

The room, collectively, exhaled.

Chapter Twenty-five

✦

Julianne shuffled downstairs in her pajamas, stretching. It had been a few days since Remi had nearly broken their door down with his surprise visit, but she was still exhausted from all the excitement. As she walked into the living room, en route to the kitchen for a bowl of cereal, she noticed Chloe perched on the edge of the sofa. Her sister was holding a brilliant orange Gerbera daisy.

"Oooh! What's this?" Julianne squealed. "Did the new boy send it over?"

"Nope, this one's for you." Chloe handed the flower to her very surprised sister. "It arrived this morning," she said with a wink, before walking away.

Julianne gingerly opened the note attached to the pretty flower.

> *Julianne, I have a surprise for you. Meet*
> *me at 8:30 tonight, at the spot where you set*
> *up your afternoon easel. I'm a very tempera-*
> *mental note, so you'd better do it my way or*
> *my feelings will be hurt.*

Julianne laughed—she'd never had a piece of stationery make demands on her before. Her interest was decidedly piqued.

By 8:30 that evening, Julianne was ready to burst with excitement and anticipation. She grabbed the flower and the note and headed down to the appointed spot on the beach. She thought about all the afternoons she'd spent in this exact spot, baking and squinting in the sun as she tried to recreate her mother's light exactly. In retrospect, those had been some great afternoons.

As she approached her destination, she noticed an easel—almost exactly like hers—set up where she used to paint. The top was draped in a sheet, and another note was attached. Julianne hesitated. So much had happened so quickly. They were staying in their house; school was starting soon. Did she really need any more surprises? Staring at the mysterious gift, though, Julianne couldn't stand the suspense and finally leaned down and opened the note tentatively. *Open me!* was all it said. Julianne laughed, thinking that she certainly would have uncovered the easel, no matter what the note had said.

She lifted the cover off to find a wrapped package. Then she went to work, gingerly peeling off the wrapping paper, layer by layer. At the end of all the unwrapping, Jules gasped. She squeezed her eyes shut and held them closed for a very long moment, breathing in and out slowly. But when she opened them again, Julianne was still shocked to find her mother's painting—*her* painting—sitting securely on the easel, restored and good as new. Except it wasn't the same landscape she'd painstakingly finished all those weeks ago. It was totally new. Much of the warped oil paint had been expertly restored, but in other parts, the mangled oils had been completely replaced. All along the painted beach, someone had worked in fragments of Julianne's latest photo session. It was the same beach scene, but with black-and-white, color, and sepia-toned photographs mingling with the oil paint. At one end of the panorama, texture had been added with actual beach sand. Pieces of sea glass and crushed pearl had been pressed seamlessly into Julianne's raging painted waves. It was absolutely amazing. It was one hundred percent Julianne while still maintaining her mother's vision. Julianne could hardly breathe, it was so beautiful.

"Do you like it?"

Jules turned around to find Remi standing there. He slid down in the sand and wrapped his arms around her.

"But . . . but, how did you?" Julianne managed to start.

Remi smiled, his dark eyes shining at Julianne. "Your dad and Chloe helped. I came by without my parents and they let me take the canvas," he said matter-of-factly.

Julianne shook her head in disbelief.

"I know a guy who restores fine art for some of Dawson and Dawson's clients," Remi continued. "Chloe gave me duplicates of your photos," he added. "I hope it's okay. I hope I didn't ruin it." Julianne could hear a tinge of concern in his voice.

"Oh, Remi, it's gorgeous!" she breathed, settling back into his embrace. "It's a million times better than I ever could have hoped for!"

"Well," Remi demurred softly, his voice sounding shy all of a sudden. "I just thought that maybe—the same way the original painting was a combination of you and your mom—maybe this painting could be a work of art that you and I are both part of." He paused. "Something beautiful that we've worked on and struggled with and built together."

Julianne felt her breath catch in her throat. She looked at the gorgeous picture in front of her—Remi was right, they had built it together. Then she gazed out at the beach and the ocean beyond the canvas and sighed happily. She leaned farther into Remi's arms and knew that, a hundred yards behind him, her family was sitting in their beautiful house looking out onto the same

beach. She and Remi had saved her home together and
built something incredibly special in the process.
Julianne turned. Looking into Remi's huge, brown eyes
she saw the reflection of the ocean as he gazed into her
face.

"Here's to building more," she whispered, as she
pulled him into a kiss.

What happens when Maddy's perfect summer
turns into her worst nightmare? Something unexpected and . . . fun?

Keep reading for a sneak peek of Hailey Abbott's
THE OTHER BOY

With the beat of a Gwen Stefani song pounding in her ears, Madeline Sinclaire clipped up her long blond hair and slid into the hot tub on her parents' deck. Steam rose up from the bubbling water, momentarily obscuring her friends' faces. She inhaled deeply and eased downward. Suddenly, something grabbed her feet under the water.

"Brian!" Maddy screamed.

Her boyfriend's sleek, wet head surfaced next to her, and everyone burst into laughter.

"What? Did I scare you?" Brian Kilburn asked, flashing his sexy little smile that curled just the edges of his mouth. After dating him for almost a year, Maddy still thought he was the cutest boy she'd ever seen. Brian's sleepy blue eyes could always melt her annoyance.

"Yes, you did, jerk!" Maddy said playfully. She punched him on his well-toned arm.

"Don't hurt him too badly," Morgan Gainsley called from the other side of the hot tub. "He's the only one left who knows how to tap a keg—Dave already passed out." She pointed to a dark shape lying in a heap on a lounge chair, barely visible through the San Francisco night.

"How is that possible?" Maddy giggled at her best friend. "The party just got started!"

"She's not going to hurt me," Brian growled. "Not before I . . ." He trailed off as he stood up in the water, grabbed Maddy, and tilted her back in his arms.

"Eeek!" She giggled, hoping she wasn't flashing the rest of the hot tub. Her D&G string bikini top didn't allow for a lot of gymnastics.

Brian went for her neck like a vampire. He started to run his mouth lower, but Maddy struggled upright and shoved him away.

"Okay, hornball. Save it for later," she said with a laugh.

Reluctantly, Brian released her and sat down again. Maddy settled back contentedly in the hot water, Brian's arm around her tanned shoulders. Light spilled over the deck from the open French doors behind her. The glow reached the manicured gardens at the edge of the two-acre lawn. Most of Richmond Country Day's upperclassmen, plastic cups of Miller High Life in hand, were packed into Maddy's living room, where the leather furniture had been pushed against the walls to make a dance floor.

On the deck, couples were cuddling on lounge chairs with beer bottles strewn on the ground next to them. Rob Davis had started a game of drunken tackle football on the lawn. "Touchdown!" a huge, hairy guy screamed as he grabbed the ball and landed headfirst in the shrubbery at the side of the yard.

Maddy smiled. Her first official house party of the summer was only an hour old, and she could already tell it was going to be a great night. In fact, it was going to be a great *summer*—maybe the best ever.

Maddy's other best friend, Kirsten Owens, slid up next to her. "So when did your parents leave?" Kirsten asked, resting her elbows on the edge of the tub behind her, looking sleek and athletic in her navy blue Speedo. Maddy laughed. Even though Kirsten's idea of a relaxing Saturday was running a ten-mile race, Maddy still found it funny that she insisted on wearing a one-piece suit to a party full of bikinis and boys.

"This afternoon—*finally*," Maddy replied. "They should be arriving in Napa any minute now."

"I cannot believe you have the house to yourself for

two whole months!" Morgan squealed, splashing across the tub to join the other two girls.

"I know, right?" Maddy agreed. "You know, at first, they actually tried to tell me that I had to help them fix up that little midlife crisis—I mean, *vineyard*. But they couldn't resist my powers of persuasion—"

"And that A in AP English, you nerd," Brian teased.

She gave Brian a push. "Go get me another beer," she ordered playfully, admiring the muscles of his back as he climbed out of the hot tub and shook the water out of his dark hair. A tan line showed where the waist of his baggy navy trunks had dropped down a little. She heaved a sigh of delight as she thought of her and Brian—and her big, empty house—together, all summer.

"Girls, we're going to have so much fun!" she declared, stretching out her long legs and watching her toes bob in the bubbling water as her two best friends flanked her on either side. "First of all, we finally got to throw the party we've been planning since finals. And for the rest of the summer, we'll have shopping in Noe Valley, the beach every afternoon—"

"Parties at your place every weekend!" Morgan finished for her, sending a splash of steaming water toward each of the girls. "You have the best party house in San Francisco, Maddy."

"No question," Kirsten said, looking across the artfully lit pool to the view of the bay. Behind them the sprawling six-bedroom Spanish-style house pulsed with Rihanna's latest album.

Maddy smiled her agreement. Everyone was getting what they wanted: Mom and Dad were living their dream up in Napa, and *she* was experiencing sweet independence down here in the city.

"I should probably go mingle, guys," she told everyone. "I *am* the hostess, after all."

Brian splashed back into the tub next to her just in time to catch her last words. "Don't go too far," he said, winking at her meaningfully. Maddy laughed at him and pulled herself onto the deck, knowing he was enjoying watching the water run off her slim, tanned figure.

"If you tap that new keg, I might have a special treat for you later," she said flirtatiously.

He grinned back. "Wait, I want my party favor right now!" He grabbed for her, but she dodged his grasp and draped a silk sarong around her hips, slipping a gauzy linen shirt on top.

As Maddy made her way to the foyer, she saw Brian's best friend push through the oak front door. "Mad-e-line!" Chad yelled, crushing her with a bear hug. The hall filled up with huge, brawny boys lugging an extra case of beer. Two skinny blondes appeared behind them, each waving a bottle of vodka. Maddy shook her head— for two of the richest girls at school, Taylor and Sunny certainly managed to look remarkably cheap.

"We brought Grey Goose!" Sunny called.

"Your place is *so* awesome, Maddy!" Taylor squealed.

"Thanks," Maddy said. "Why don't you stick the vodka in the kitchen?"

"Oh my God, is that *Scott Winters*?" Sunny screeched in reply, staring into the living room. "Doesn't he play for UCLA?" She and Taylor hustled past Maddy, nearly knocking her over.

Within an hour, her house was filled with basically every person she knew—and a bunch she didn't. Maddy felt like the queen of summer. When she looked around again, Morgan and Kirsten were dramatically debating something with Taylor. Sunny was making out with a guy from Cathedral Prep. Someone had put on the Ying Yang Twins, and couples were grinding in the living room and making out on the sofas. Rob Davis broke a Lalique vase, and Maddy was drinking vodka tonics *way* too fast.

She needed a breather. So she made her way back onto the now-deserted deck, trying not to stumble too much. "Mmmm," she murmured, collapsing onto a canvas lounge chair. She closed her eyes and let the pounding music behind her wash through her mind. She could feel someone standing over her.

"I've come to collect my party favor now, hostess," Brian whispered as he slid onto the chair next to her. Maddy smiled and wrapped her arms around his neck.

He pulled her on top of him. "I am so glad your parents are gone."

"Me too." She loved the feeling of his whole body pressed against hers. She twined her fingers in the wavy hair at the back of his head and kissed him gently. His body tensed, and excitement shot through her. Mmm. Brian was so yummy. His lips always tasted like cinnamon.

He wrapped his arms around her and flipped himself over, taking her with him. Now he was on top, gazing down at her. "It's going to be a great summer, Madeline Sinclaire," he said softly as he pressed his hips against hers. She closed her eyes and he kissed her again, this time parting her lips with his tongue.

I couldn't agree more, she thought. She ran her hands up and down his bare back under his T-shirt as he shifted to the side a little and slid her shirt up. She shivered at the sensation of the fabric brushing her skin.

After a few blissful minutes, Maddy drew back and glanced at the diamond-encrusted Bulgari tank watch her parents had given her for her sixteenth birthday. Ten o'clock. Mom and Dad would have unloaded all the wheelbarrows and pitchforks and whatever the hell they used to resuscitate a run-down vineyard by now and be sipping wine, happily oblivious to the biggest party in Sea Cliff. "I should probably go make sure no one's throwing chairs out of windows or something," she said.

Brian groaned and reached for her.

"Don't leave yet."

She smiled and tried to pull him up. "Come with me!"

The packed living room was grinding to the heavy bass line. The crowd had spilled up the stairs—Maddy could hear some sort of thumping from her parents' room overhead—and into the kitchen.

"Rob, what are you doing in there?" Maddy called over to the brawny football player. Rob Davis had apparently given up on running around the yard and had just taken the top off of the blender.

"A little something I like to call Robbie's Late Night Bean Special," Rob answered with a grin. "You'll love it, Sinclaire."

The whir of the blender was just audible over the music. In the very back of her mind, Maddy briefly wondered if he was trashing the kitchen but decided it didn't matter. After all, she had two whole months to clean up, and right now, dancing to Beyoncé was her main priority. *Your love's got me looking so crazy right now.*

Brian's arm slid around her waist. He pulled her up tightly against him and handed her a cold beer from the freshly tapped keg. Maddy wrapped one arm around his shoulders, swaying her hips to the music, and took a sip with the other hand. "Mmmm," she murmured and buried her face in his neck. *Your touch got me looking so crazy right now.*

From behind her, she could hear Morgan shrieking, "Oh my God! She did not!" Somewhere, glass shattered. Maddy shook her hair back from her face and raised her arms in the air, swaying to the music. Brian took her chin in his hand and leaned down.

"You're the most beautiful girl I've ever seen," he murmured into her ear, his lips brushing the side of her face. Their eyes met as he slowly brought his mouth to hers.

Maddy felt like her whole body was electrified. She ran her hands down Brian's back as he dipped her backward.

"Ow! Ow! Go Maddy!" Kirsten giggled, bumping her shoulder.

Maddy twirled around, her eyes closed, singing as loud as she could, "*Got me looking so crazy in love!*"

In the distance, she could hear someone calling her name. But the music drowned out the voice. She'd deal with it when this song ended. Beyoncé could not be ignored. Then the call came closer.

"Maddy! Madeline Sinclaire!"

That sounds like my father, she thought dreamily. *I wonder if they even have stereos in Napa.*

"MADELINE! SINCLAIRE!"

Wow, that really does sound like Dad. Maddy smiled to herself. But when she opened her eyes, her father was not smiling back.

Steamy summer reads

Forbidden Boy

When Julianne falls for Remi at a bonfire party, it looks like her summer is off to a perfect start. Then she discovers that her awful new neighbors are Remi's parents, making him a forbidden boy. But what do you do when your worst enemy is also the boy of your dreams?

The Other Boy

When she gets caught throwing a party, Maddy's parents force her to spend the summer with them, hours away from her boyfriend. But things start looking up after she meets David. When they realize they share a passion for cooking, will love start with the very first bite?

The Perfect Boy

When AJ, a hot rapper, shows interest in Heidi instead of her, Ciara and her friend Kevin devise a plan to help her win AJ over. But the closer Ciara gets to Kevin, the more she wonders, who really is the perfect boy?

HARPER TEEN
An Imprint of HarperCollins Publishers

by Hailey Abbott!

Waking Up to Boys

Chelsea's more comfortable strapped onto her wakeboard than flirting with Todd, the adorable watersports instructor she's been crushing on for years. So she concentrates on winning this summer's Northwest Extreme Watersports Competition. That is, until hot, Brazilian Sebastian wakes her up to the fact that she can get a boy. But can she get the one she really wants, even if she's competing against him for the gold?

The Secrets of Boys

A California girl like Cassidy should be out on the beach with her boyfriend, not stuck in summer school! But her life heats up when she meets the worldly and romantic Zach. Will temptation be too strong to resist?

Getting Lost with Boys

When Jacob offers to drive with her to her sister's place in Northern California, Cordelia's neatly laid out summer plans quickly turn into a wild road trip, where anything can—and does—happen. Who knew getting lost with a boy could be so much fun?

Don't miss the

Shey

What happens when a good girl teams up with a total player and creates the biggest scandal their school has ever seen?

When popular guy Camden convinces Maya the only way to save her family's Thai restaurant is to do other kids' homework for cash, she soon finds out that everything has a price. Especially falling in love.